Daisy Morrow, Super-sleuth!

The Third One:

A Very Unexpected African Adventure

R T GREEN
and Ann Nassolo

Other books...

The Daisy Morrow Series:

The first one – The Root of All Evil
The second one – The Strange Case of the Exploding Dolly-trolley
The third one – A Very Unexpected African Adventure
The fourth one - Pirates of Great Yarmouth: Curse of the Crimson Heart
The sixth one – Call of Duty: The Wiltingham Enigma
The Box Set – books 1-3

Pale Moon: Season 1:

Episode 1: Rising
Episode 2: Falling
Episode 3: Broken
Episode 4: Phoenix
Episode 5: Jealousy
Episode 6: Homecoming
Episode 7: Fearless
Episode 8: Infinity

Season 2:

Episode 9: Phantom
Episode 10: Endgame
Episode 11: Desperation
Episode 12: Feral
Episode 13: Unbreakable
Episode 14: Phenomenal
Episode 15: Newborn
Episode 16: Evermore

The Starstruck Series -

Starstruck: Somewhere to call Home
Starstruck: The Prequel

(Time to say Goodbye)
Starstruck: The Disappearance of Becca
Starstruck: The Rock
Starstruck: Ghosts, Ghouls and Evil Spirits
Starstruck: The Combo – books 1-3

The Raven Series –

Raven: No Angel!
Raven: Unstoppable
Raven: Black Rose
Raven: The Combo – books 1-3

Little Cloud
Timeless
Ballistic
Cry of an Angel
The Hand of Time
Wisp
The Standalones

A Dedication from Richard

Although Ann helped write this book, I'm still going to dedicate it to her, with much love and respect.

Her Ugandan eyes have been invaluable in making this book as authentic as possible, with only the bare minimum of 'artistic licence'.

My grateful thanks and appreciation x

Contents

COME AND JOIN US!

We'd love you to become a VIP Reader.

Our intro library is the most generous in publishing!
Join our mail list and grab it all for free.
We really do appreciate every single one of you,
so there's always a freebie or two coming along,
news and updates, advance reads of new releases...

Head here to get started...
rtgreen.net

Introduction

This is the third book in the Daisy Morrow series. As you might have seen from the first two, our R.E.D. heroine is nothing like you might expect; she's funny, feisty, and has a tendency to get herself in sticky situations. And she definitely has a wicked side!

Before she retired, Daisy had a job very few people ever have, and although in the last few years she's done her best to leave her legacy behind, somehow it manages to keep lurking in the shadows... in more ways than one!

Those of you who know our work will be aware that with the RTG brand, the unexpected is always around the next corner. Daisy is no exception, and very probably has even more corners.

This time Daisy, Aidan and Sarah are in Africa, but that doesn't stop the fun and games. It seems no matter where she goes, trouble finds her... even when it means she's one step away from causing an international incident!

A big element of the story revolves around an actual incident that took place in Uganda in 1964. The murder itself is, of course, fictitious, but the rest of it did actually happen. And in line with most RTG books, the majority of the locations you'll visit are real too... even down to the street names. If they're mentioned in the book, and you have an idle moment to meander around Google maps, you will find them!

We hope Daisy will make you smile, and maybe even gasp in surprise and shake your head a little. If she does, that will make us happy people!

Please let us know what you think, either by email, or ideally by writing a review. Every comment is gratefully received... and is listened to!

Enjoy,
Richard and Ann

How the Second One ended...

Daisy watched DCI Burrows' eyes as he read the statement he'd asked her and Aidan to compile. Sitting on the opposite side of the desk in his office, she waited patiently for him to finish.

He dropped it back on the desk, and shook his head in the despairing way she'd got used to seeing. 'You really are a pain in my butt, Daisy Morrow.'

'I know, Inspector. But just think what life would be like without us in it.'

'Oh trust me, I often do. But somehow you seem to come out of it smelling of roses each time. Or daisies maybe.'

Aidan, sitting next to Daisy, laughed. 'Just be grateful, Inspector. I have to smell the daisies every day!'

Daisy scowled at him, but there was a smile on her face. 'So what's the upshot of it all?'

Burrows had a hint of a smile on his craggy face. 'Well, Adde Wambua can't be prosecuted because he's not here anymore. Some would say he got his just desserts.'

'That includes Aidan and me.'

'I'm sure it does. But thanks to you two and Officer Lowry acting in an *unofficial* capacity, Belgian police are going to bring Carmella deBruin to justice. The videos you secretly made aren't strictly-speaking admissible in court, but combined with the dried blood evidence you *finally* admitted to finding, there isn't much doubt she will go away for a very long time.'

'Sarah only kept it from you because I begged her to, Inspector. I realise she, um... bent protocol a bit, but I hope you can see the greater good. Will she be punished at all?'

He stood up, walked to the window and stood looking out with his hands in his pockets. 'I *should* punish her. But on the other hand, her work and her initiative resulted in bringing two criminals to justice. So am I biting off the hand that feeds me, Daisy?'

'If you punish her, you will be, Inspector.'

He turned back into the room. 'I had a feeling you were going to say that.'

'Of course we were,' said Aidan. 'She's the best thing that's ever happened to you.'

He sat down again, and smiled. 'I'll take that with a pinch of hot curry sauce, Aidan.'

Daisy had something else on her mind. 'It's been three days now, Inspector, and she's still beating herself up about what happened at the end. Even though she only did what she had to, and because I had the shakes and couldn't. I think she needs a little time to recover.'

His eyes clouded over. 'Me too. She's still a rookie cop, and things like that can affect an inexperienced officer for years... sometimes for ever. I suppose you have a suggestion?'

'As it happens...'

'Why did I get the feeling you were going to say that?'

'She needs a break, time to pull herself back together. And she saved our lives when even we thought no one would. We'd like to take Sarah and ourselves away for a couple of weeks... a little holiday to say thank you and fix her back up.'

He nodded like he understood. 'Ok. When?'

'As soon as we can book the flights. In the next few days for sure.'

'So be it. I'll authorise the time off, on medical grounds. I'll leave it to you to do the rest.'

Daisy and Aidan walked through the squad room on their way out, paused at Sarah's desk. 'We're going to do a little shopping in the city, and then grab some lunch. You want to join us?'

'I'll have to see if it's okay with Burrows.'

Daisy put a hand on her shoulder. 'It'll be fine, trust me. Call you when we're ready to eat.'

They spent an hour shopping in the Kings Lynn mall, and then Aidan was looking like he'd had enough. In truth, Daisy felt the same. It had only been three days since their ordeal by seawater, and Sarah wasn't the only one who needed recovery time.

The trip to the city had really only been made for one reason. The statement Daisy and Aidan had written had been worded in such a way to make sure Sarah couldn't be blamed for anything. Burrows hadn't been on their back about getting it to him, it could just as easily have been posted in.

Taking it to him in person had been an excuse to make sure he gave Sarah time off. That was important to Daisy and Aidan, and there was more than one reason for that too.

Sarah grinned as she walked into the restaurant and found the two of them waiting for her at a red plastic table. 'I thought this would be the last place you'd want to be!'

'Hey, I'm taking Aidan here for our anniversary next time,' Daisy grinned.

He laughed, but there was a genuine sense of relief in it. 'Let's face it, if it hadn't been for McDonald's fat straws, we wouldn't be here now!'

Sarah couldn't help a shudder racking her body. 'Tell me about it.'

Daisy stood up quickly. 'Ok, enough of that. Let's go and get food.'

She slipped an arm into Sarah's, and marched her to the counter. Five minutes later they were back with a tray full of burgers and fries.

Sarah unwrapped her Big Tasty. 'So, how did it go with the boss?'

'Fine. He's fully exonerated you of any criminal proceedings,' Daisy grinned.

'I suppose that's something,' Sarah said, looking less than pleased.

'And he thinks you should take time off to recover.'

'Oh... I'm fine. I'm a survivor.'

'So are we, apparently. But you're not fine. Trust me, I know.'

'Maybe you'll tell me how you know one day.'

'One day, dear. But right now, it's all arranged.'

'What is?'

'Your time off.'

Sarah narrowed her eyes. 'Daisy, what did you do?'

'Nothing... well, we just suggested we all go away on a little holiday, to say thank you to you for us actually being able to have one.'

'And Burrows said yes?'

'Of course. He's not such a bad old stick really.'

'Wow... I suppose I could do with a break. So where are we going?'

'Africa!' Daisy and Aidan said together.

'How did I know you were going to say that?'

'Don't you start.'

The burgers were eaten, and Sarah decided she wanted another hot chocolate. She stood up to head for the serving counter. 'You guys want another drink?'

Daisy and Aidan looked at each other, their telepathic link kicking in. Daisy grinned. 'Sure... anything that doesn't need a straw!'

———

And now The Third one:

A Very Unexpected African Adventure

Chapter 1

'This is so exciting!'

'Everything is exciting to you,' smiled Daisy, sitting next to Sarah, in the aisle seat.

'Yes, but I've not led your dramatic life,' she said, tearing her eyes away from the window and grinning back.

'Give it time, dear… you're getting there.'

Sarah, unable to not look out of the window for more than a second, watched as the airliner turned in a gentle bank to prepare for its final approach, and the lights of the runway at Entebbe airport filled her view.

'Oh.'

'Oh?'

'Um… what happens if we overshoot the landing? The runway seems to end right before the sea.'

'Lake dear, lake.'

'Well it looks like the sea… and it can drown you just as easily.'

Daisy patted her on the leg. 'Never mind dear, Aidan and me have had enough almost-drownings in recent weeks. We certainly wouldn't willingly put all our lives in danger.'

Aidan, sitting in the sear right behind them, poked his head through and grinned cheekily. 'And why do you think we took out travel insurance?'

'You're not exactly helping, Aidan.'

Daisy noticed the genuine look of concern on Sarah's face. 'Dear, it just doesn't happen, so take no notice of my lovely husband doing his best to wind you up. And anyway, if we do overshoot, the pilot just opens the throttles and we lift off again.'

'Still not helping, Daisy.'

'Sarah dear, just relax. There are plenty of buoyancy jackets.'

Sarah shook her head, and went back to watching the descent. The Emirates flight had taken fourteen hours in total with a short stop in Addis Ababa, so they were all more than ready to stretch their legs. For Sarah and Aidan, it was the first time they'd been to Africa, but Daisy had been before, three times in the distant past. But not to Uganda, so from that perspective it was an *exciting* new adventure for them all.

It had been a fraught seven days; the flights had been purchased straight away, but the Yellow Fever jabs and visas had taken several days to organise. Much to Daisy's impatience... if she'd had her way they would have been on a flight the day after she'd persuaded Burrows to grant Sarah time off.

The unexpected truth Adde Wambua let slip before his death was a much stronger lead than they'd ever had in helping to solve Celia's disappearance. In the space of three days before he died they'd discovered he was the one responsible for trafficking their daughter, and that she'd been sold to someone in Uganda.

He genuinely didn't know who, but he did know he was a high ranking government official. Which didn't help Daisy's cause. In Museveni's Uganda, such officials were almost always military, and protected by the army's rules of

22

privacy. Everyone else got to know only what he wanted them to.

Extracting Celia from such a regime would not be easy, even if they could find out who it was who'd actually bought her.

They'd booked flights home for two weeks time, just because they needed to show the Ugandan customs officials they had a return flight booked. But none of them knew if two weeks would be enough. The visas lasted forty-five days, and it might well be that return flights would have to be rebooked.

Both Aidan and Sarah knew Daisy would not go back to the UK until they'd found Celia. Even if she ended up having to stay there illegally.

The aircraft didn't overshoot the runway and end up at the bottom of Lake Victoria. As it taxied to the concourse outside the main building in the late-afternoon sunshine, Sarah gathered up her tablet, and looked at Daisy with wide eyes and flushed cheeks.

'I can't believe we're actually here!'

'Don't get too excited yet... we still have to endure a taxi-ride to Kampala.'

Aidan put a hand on her shoulder as they joined the disembarkation queue, and smiled reassuringly. 'Don't worry, Sarah. That main road is all asphalt, so as long as the driver avoids the potholes, we'll be alright.'

'And there was me thinking we'd be in the back of a cattle-truck.'

'Ok, point taken. I'll shut up now.'

Entebbe International Airport was actually quite smart. Way smaller than their departure point at Heathrow, it didn't really have any vast spaces with high ceilings. Much of it had been rebuilt just a few years ago, and their route through customs was quick and accompanied by big, friendly smiles. As they collected their luggage, Daisy slapped dry lips together.

'I'd love a coffee, dear. Look, the Crane Cafe is just over there. If it's ok to have ten minutes before we find a taxi, would you and Sarah grab drinks? I need the loo before taking in any more liquid.'

'Sounds like a plan. Come on Sarah... get a few Ugandan shillings out!'

Daisy headed to the toilets, but three minutes later, just as she was hurrying back to join the others, someone caught her eye. He looked Ugandan, middle-aged, and not very well. Dressed in a cream suit and patterned shirt, as she watched he staggered slightly.

No one else noticed the man. The speakers had just announced boarding for the next flight to Nairobi, and most of the people in the waiting area were already hurrying to the gate. The man seemed like he was intending to join them, but he was a little way behind the crowd, and his legs looked like they were just about to collapse under him.

He grabbed the wall to hold himself up, but it wasn't enough. He fell to his knees. Daisy ran over to him. Still no one else was close by. Fifteen feet from the exit doors, he must have entered through them just a minute or two before, on his way to catch his flight. He had no luggage she could see, not even a hand-held case.

She knelt down beside him and reached out a hand, curled it around his shoulder. As he looked up to her with heavy eyes, she could feel his whole body shaking.

'Please...' he gasped in a soft Ugandan accent.

'Let me call someone,' said Daisy, realising he was in a bad way.

24

'No... no police...' he whispered, the corners of his mouth turning down as speaking became just as hard as moving.

'What can I do?' Daisy cried frantically.

He found a little movement, slipped a trembling hand into the pocket of his jacket. It looked like it was all he could do. And then he thrust a crumpled piece of paper into her hand, tried to say something.

The words wouldn't come. He let out a croaky kind of gasp, and one second later was flat out on the floor.

Daisy pressed a finger onto his neck, just as Aidan and Sarah came running up. 'Oh my god...' cried Sarah. 'Is he..?'

Daisy nodded. 'Yes, he's dead.'

Aidan looked around for some kind of divine inspiration. 'How long have we been here, dear?' Then he shook his head despondently. 'I'll find someone.'

A couple of airport police officers were already heading their way. Aidan met them, gave them the news. Before they reached the dead man, Daisy took a quick look at the note, and then shoved it hastily into her pocket.

'What's that?' whispered Sarah.

'Don't say anything yet, please? It was important enough for him to give it to me as his last act. It's just a name and a date, but it clearly means something.'

'You should give it to the police, Daisy.'

'I know. But he begged me not to involve the police. We need to find out who he is, and why this was so crucial to him.'

'So you're telling me we've only been on African soil for an hour, and already there are two mysteries to solve, not one?'

'Yes dear, it rather looks that way.'

Chapter 2

The slightly portly but not very tall police officer looked at Daisy over the top of his thick-rimmed spectacles. 'So what is your connection to this man?'

Daisy shook her head, realising it was an obvious question that didn't have an easy-to-explain answer. 'We have no connection, officer. We are just here for a short holiday.'

'And yet my officers found you kneeling over a dying man, Mrs. Henderson?'

Daisy groaned inwardly. 'I know it looks bad... sir, but I can assure you he simply staggered over to me, before dying at my feet. What was I supposed to do?'

'Hmm...' His eyes dropped back to the passport in his hands. He flicked the pages in an idle kind of way, like he was looking for something that wasn't there. 'I see you have visited Africa before.'

'Yes, but not Uganda. I visited Kenya, a long time ago.'

'So I see.' Still he didn't look like he was in any hurry to make a decision. Daisy glanced over to Aidan and Sarah, sitting on hard chairs a few feet away. The small room held little apart from the desk and a few chairs, and was obviously the place they took visitors they didn't like the look of.

Or those associated with men who died on the premises.

The officer in charge picked up a second passport, which had an airline ticket slipped inside it. Then he pierced a glare into Daisy again. 'Do you know why this man was flying to Nairobi, Mrs. Henderson?'

'I didn't even know that's where he was going. I told you, he is a total stranger to me.'

Aidan spoke up. 'What was his name, please?'

The officer hesitated, and then sat back in his padded chair, turning the pages of the man's passport. 'His name was Ssebina Michael.'

'That's an unusual first name.'

Daisy smiled to Aidan. 'It's his surname, dear. In Uganda the family name comes first.' Then she looked away and swallowed hard, trying not to look like she was. It was the second time she'd come across that surname in less than two hours. She forced a smile. 'May we go now, officer?'

He nodded his head slowly. 'It does not appear there was any obvious wrong-doing on your part. But I need to know where are you staying?'

'We have rooms booked at the Imperial Royale in Kampala. We'd like to get there as soon as possible, please.'

A young man walked into the room, nodded silently to his boss, who seemed to know what it meant. 'Very well. My staff have examined your suitcases, and found nothing to lead us to believe you are a threat. You may continue on your journey for now... but we may wish to talk to you again.'

Sarah spoke as she got to her feet. 'Can you tell us what the man died of, please?'

He shook his head. 'There are no outward signs of what may have killed him. His body is now being picked up, to be taken to the hospital in Kampala to undergo a post-mortem. That may reveal how he died, but it was likely a heart attack.'

'Will you let us know, please?' asked Daisy.

He nodded again, indicated the door to his guests. They filed through, to find their luggage waiting for them in the corridor. Daisy blew out her cheeks to Aidan and Sarah.

'Welcome to Uganda, dears.'

The early-evening air of the forecourt was a kind of relief, even though it was a lot warmer than the air-conditioned but stifling atmosphere of the detainee's interrogation room. They seemed to be the only ones standing there, their fellow international passengers long since gone.

Just about to start walking to find a taxi, Daisy covered her ears with her hands as Sarah stuck two fingers in her mouth and let out a screeching whistle.

'What the hell are you doing? That might work in the centre of Kings Lynn, but nobody here will take a blind bit of notice of…'

The sentence died away, as a tatty old Nissan minibus screeched to a halt in front of them, proving her completely wrong.

A young man who didn't look old enough to drive legally jumped out, flashed them a wide grin, and grabbed their luggage before they had chance to change their minds. 'Wilfred at your service. Where can I take you?'

'Um… the Imperial Royale in Kampala, please,' said a slightly-bemused Daisy.

Wilfred wasn't focusing right then on the older members of the party. The dazzling smile was aimed straight at Sarah, as was the hand that reached out to her arm, making sure she was safely escorted to the seat in the front of the bus. Only then did he open the rear door and wave his other passengers into their seats with a chauffeur-like flourish.

Daisy looked at Aidan with a slightly-nervous smile.

'Don't worry, dear. I think Sarah can take care of herself,' he said.

They'd only just passed under the roof of the airport exit checkpoint when Wilfred went to work.

'Do you have a name, pretty muzungu?'

'Of course I have a name.'

The dazzle faded for a moment. But only a moment. 'I would like to know it, please.'

'It's Sarah.'

'Ah. What a beautiful name, for a beautiful mu... woman. Maybe we explore the nightlife sometime very soon? I make a good guide, and I got plenty to offer you.'

'Seriously?'

'Sure, Sarah. We have some fun... let your grandparents chill, yes?'

'I'm sorry?'

'Your grandparents? They need lots of rest, I think.'

Daisy couldn't bite her lip any longer, even though Sarah seemed to be doing a good job of holding her own. She leant forward between the seats. 'We're not her grandparents. We're her minders.'

The minibus slewed across the road as Wilfred's brain took in the words. 'M... *minders?*'

Sarah threw him a cheesy smile. 'That's right. My minders.'

Wilfred's predatory spirit faded a little for the next half-mile. But after that, he still couldn't help himself. Sarah watched as his hand left the steering wheel and dropped to the seat, dangerously close to the part of her thigh the rather short shorts weren't covering. The hand was accompanied by the dazzle, and a few more words.

'Hey, beautiful lady. It don't matter, we can still make our own fun, if you get me?'

The hand looked like it was itching to make home base. Sarah tried to match the smile. 'Oh Wilfred, that's so

29

tempting. But doesn't a handsome young boy like you have a girlfriend? Or aren't you old enough?'

'Hey... that ain't called for. I can easily show you how old I am... look, I even got business cards.'

The hand momentarily broke its journey to the thigh, fumbled in the open storage box between the seats. He handed her a small white card.

Sarah read the words written on it, let out a giggle. 'Will.i.is? Taking you places you ain't never been before?'

'Clever, huh?'

'Genius.'

He seemed to miss the sarcasm. The hand resumed its creeping journey towards the thigh. Out of the corner of her eye, Sarah watched it drift ever nearer.

'Anyway, I'm too busy for fun. I'm here on business, not for pleasure.'

'Business? You a receptionist or something?'

'No. I'm a police officer. And if you lay one finger on me, I'll break all ten of them.'

The hand promptly flew back to the wheel, and gripped it a little more firmly than it had ever done before.

Chapter 3

'I thought you said Uganda was a poor country?'

Daisy wrapped her hand around Aidan's, let out a little chuckle. 'It is, but we're right in Museveni country now. This is where a lot of the other half live… well, the other five percent anyway.' She pointed through the side window, across manicured lawns bordered by elegant low walls. 'That's State House, where he lives.'

Aidan strained to see the huge white building half a mile away. 'Wow… it makes our cottage look like a tent in a field!'

'Yes dear… but at least we don't have a few hundred troops guarding the place.'

'One or two might be nice though.'

They were driving quite slowly along the part of Portal Road that was dual-carriageway. The up-market part of Entebbe with its lush green lawns and tall streetlamps looked almost like an elegant suburb of outer London, except for the palm trees dotting the sides of the road.

Pretty much every sign they saw was in English, and the road they were travelling was smooth asphalt. She noticed Aidan shake his head slightly. 'Don't worry dear, I'm sure you'll see plenty of real Ugandan street-life before we go home.'

Then she noticed most of the vehicles on the road seemed to be overtaking them, so leant forward and tapped their young driver on the shoulder. 'Wilfred, you don't *have* to drive so slowly. We know the deal, but we'll give you a fair price for the ride. We would like to get there before midnight!'

Wilfred jumped like she'd given him an electric shock. 'Sure… sure thing, lady boss,' he said nervously, and then put his foot down a little harder.

Ten minutes later they were in open countryside. Aidan's gaze was still fixed firmly through the window, even though it was almost dark. 'It's quite beautiful here. I didn't realise how hilly it was.'

'Bit different to Norfolk, hey Dip?'

'*Now* I'm getting the feeling I'm in a foreign country.'

'Apparently there are seven official hills in Kampala city itself. And you'll definitely know you're in a foreign country then.'

'I'd like to explore the bits the tourists don't get to see, if there's time.'

'You'll be stared at.'

'I can cope with that.'

'Most of the locals are really friendly. Just keep your wallet somewhere safe.'

'Don't worry. I've been to Wandsworth a few times!'

An hour later they screeched up a ramp and came to a halt outside the entrance to the Imperial Royale, set right in the centre of the business district of central Kampala, which kind of resembled the city of London. Aidan didn't look very impressed again.

'It doesn't look very… African.'

'Dear, if you wanted to glamp in a mud hut you should have said. There's plenty of that around outside the city.'

Wilfred was lifting the rear hatch of the Nissan, pulling out their luggage. 'You want me to carry your stuff to reception? Just a few extra shillings?'

Sarah grabbed her bag. 'No thank you. Me and the geriatrics can take it from here.'

His eyes flicked around his passengers, as his brain remembered Sarah's words. He almost looked afraid. 'Sure... sure... sorry about the, um, misunderstanding. We good now?'

'That depends what you're going to charge us.'

'Um... half a mil?'

'Seriously?

'Four hundred thousand?' he suggested hopefully.

'I'll give you two-fifty. That's still far more than you'd get normally... even from rich white muzungus.'

His eyes were still flicking around, likely something to do with the two security officers who were standing close by, idly watching them. 'Sure, sure. That's ok,' he said shakily.

Sarah handed him the Ugandan shillings. He tried to hide his delight, make it look like a resigned and reluctant acceptance of the deal he'd got, but didn't do a very good job. He disappeared into the driving seat, and the minibus drove away.

'Didn't realise you were so good at bantering,' Daisy grinned.

'You didn't see how close his hand got to my thigh,' Sarah growled back.

They headed to the hotel building, right into a security checkpoint, operated by staff with the badges of a private security company. Almost as soon as they made the entrance, three young hotel bell boys dressed in red uniforms took the luggage from them, and passed it through a scanner. They were asked to do the same, made to walk through a person-sized scanner.

'Now I *know* I'm in a foreign country,' Aidan grinned.

33

Then they were invited through into the hotel proper, and found themselves in a huge space which felt even bigger than the outside space they'd just left. Stretching above them was floor after floor of curved walkways, serving the rooms on each level. On one side of the ground floor, a huge brown granite and expensive wood reception desk was designed to look opulent, with oversized floor-standing pots of flowers and plants positioned at each end of it.

The bell boys were ahead of them, waiting with their luggage in front of the reception desk. Aidan checked them in, and the good-looking receptionist scanned their passports. Then she ran them through what they were entitled to expect with a standard room.

Daisy gazed around, taking in her surroundings. Behind the reception area was a wall full of pictures; some of Aga Khan, Museveni, and a few awards the hotel had been given. She smiled to herself... Aidan would definitely feel he was in a foreign country looking at those. The hotel was owned by Indians, and she wondered how many Brit hotels had a picture of the Queen or Boris Johnson hanging in reception!

Her eyes drifted to the far wall, which appeared to be a quarter of a mile away. A short run of brown-tiled steps led to a sitting area with sofas dotted around the space, and a big illuminated fish tank standing against one wall. Set into the far wall were the elevators to the upper floors.

Then Aidan touched her arm, bringing her back to the there-and-then. The bell boys were already scurrying up the steps, so the three of them followed to the elevators. Their rooms were on the eighth floor, and as the doors pinged aside they stepped out onto carpeted open walkways. The bell boys opened the door to the first room, beckoned them to go inside, and then followed them in and placed the luggage into a big area that seemed to have no purpose other than to contain their bags.

Daisy tipped them, and they gave her appreciative smiles and left. The room was huge... pretty much like any other hotel room, with a king-sized bed and doors that led to a balcony... but it was far bigger than any hotel room they'd ever stayed in before.

Sarah grinned. 'I didn't need my own room, I could have slept on the couch and still be a distance away from you.'

'So you'd be happy to put up with Aidan snoring like a rhino?'

'Hey... I don't snore.'

'And you know that how?'

'Well...'

Daisy tapped Sarah on the arm affectionately. 'Be thankful you've got space to yourself, dear.'

'I can hear, you know.'

Chapter 4

Sarah left to explore her room, which was right next to Daisy and Aidan's. Daisy wandered out onto the balcony, leant her elbows on the rail and gazed thoughtfully out across the view of north-east Kampala. She felt an arm around her waist, as Aidan joined her and followed her eyes.

'Looking for something, Flower?'

She turned to him, wrapped her arms around his shoulders. He could see the gloss of tears in her eyes as she spoke, almost in a whisper. 'I was just wondering if Celia was out there somewhere, and I was looking at her without realising it.'

He rested his head against hers. 'It's a big city, dear. Maybe you are, but there's no guarantee she's even in Kampala. Although I guess it's just as likely as anywhere, especially if she was bought by someone high up in the military ranks.'

'Where do we even start looking?'

He heard the desolate tone in her words, kissed her softly. 'I guess first off I rig up the laptop, try trawling the internet for names.'

'That won't be easy. But maybe Anton could help with that? He said he'd come and see us as soon as we got here. He should be arriving soon.'

A shout from the next balcony ripped Daisy away from the morbid thoughts. 'Hey, you two. My room is huge too... but there's a big crack in the ceiling!'

Aidan grinned, seeing the opportunity for another wind-up. 'Well, you know this place is built with straw walls under the plaster? We could be lucky though, it might not collapse until we're gone.'

'You winding me up again, Henderson?'

'Would I?'

'You've already proved you would, so please stop trying.'

'Guess there's no fooling an officer of the law.'

'Believe it.'

The phone in the room buzzed. Aidan answered it, and then shouted out to Daisy. 'Anton is here, waiting to meet us in the lobby.'

Daisy called across to Sarah. 'An old friend of mine is here. You want to come with us and meet him?'

'On my way.'

As the elevator doors pinged open onto the lobby area they'd walked through an hour earlier, a strange man was sitting on one of the sofas, waiting for them.

He wasn't really that strange, but he sure was an unusual sight in Uganda. As he stood up with a big beaming smile, his long brown leather coat dropped almost to the floor. Unbuttoned, it revealed the checked shirt and red braces underneath. The cowboy hat on his head matched the coat, and his long auburn hair was tied back into a ponytail, sitting behind a moustached face almost hidden by a big, bushy beard.

He looked like he could have once played lead guitar in ZZ Top, and that he'd be more at home in the hills somewhere in the American mid-west. He opened his leather-clad arms and wrapped them around Daisy, and gave all three of them a beaming smile as he boomed out a greeting in an American accent.

'Daisy, Daisy... geez, you don't look a day older, girl.'

37

She slapped both hands onto his chest. 'Give over... we haven't seen each other for forty years. Last time we met I had blonde hair.'

He winked one of his sparkly green eyes. 'But you look a hell of a lot scarier with silver hair, I gotta say.'

'Now you're just trying to flatter me.'

He lifted his hands from his sides. 'Just as sharp as ever, hun.'

Daisy turned to Aidan and Sarah. 'Guys, meet Anton Kowalski, a good friend of mine from... well, a long time ago.'

Aidan smiled, held out a hand. Daisy had told him all about the time way back when they'd briefly worked together in Mombasa, but he'd never actually met him. Anton took the hand, shook it vigorously. 'Good to meet the guy who finally tamed the lioness, Aidan. Kudos to you!'

'Well, I don't know I ever did tame her. Maybe I just managed to put a lid on her, but that has a habit of blowing off when the heat gets turned up.'

'What are you saying, dear?' Daisy tried to protest, knowing he was actually spot on.

'Nothing, dear. Nothing.'

Anton turned to Sarah, who was still staring open mouthed at the strange sight in front of her. 'And you must be Sarah. Daisy told me a lot about you and your spirit, a few days ago.'

'Really? She didn't tell me anything about you.'

'I wanted it to be a surprise, Sarah dear.'

Her mouth dropped open even further. 'Surprise? I'll say. A hillbilly? In Uganda? Named Anton Kowalski?'

He guffawed loudly, making a middle-aged couple sitting on a sofa the other side of the lobby glance over. Not that it was the first time they'd looked in his direction. 'Hillbilly...

well, I guess you kinda hit the nail on the head. I was born in cowboy country, more years ago than I care to recall.'

'And now you live in Uganda but still dress like you're in America?'

Daisy offered a part-explanation. 'Anton only lives in Uganda at weekends... he owns an island just off the coast, on Lake Victoria. Well, his wife does... foreigners aren't allowed to own property in Uganda. Weekdays he spends in Nairobi. Like me he used to be an active field operative, but now he's an old man he's been side-promoted to a desk job at the US embassy. Don't ask me where all the hair came from though... last time I saw him he looked quite normal.'

Anton guffawed again. 'Dear Daisy, I see the acid wit hasn't been diminished by the passage of time.' He indicated for them to sit. 'Truth is, when you're a white guy living in this part of the world, there are some advantages to looking different. I guess the hillbilly look kinda grew over time.'

'Like the hair and the beard?'

He grinned. 'It helps disguise the expressions when you're telling lies to the authorities.'

Sarah was still looking at him like she couldn't quite believe what she was seeing. 'Your wife... is she American too?'

'Hell no. Gave up on white girls decades ago. Enid is as Ugandan as Ugandan gets. Pretty as a picture, and even after fifteen years I still ask myself what she sees in me.'

'Maybe she's still waiting to actually *see* you?' Sarah grinned.

Anton laughed from behind the whiskers. 'Y'know gal, you could be right there.'

'And she lives on that tiny island all alone during the week?'

'Nah. Monday to Friday she stays with her sister in Masaka, helping run her shop. Weekends we retreat together.'

'Sounds like tropical heaven.'

'You bet.' He nodded to the sports bag sitting against the side of the sofa, said slightly too loudly. 'That's the swimwear you asked me to bring, Daisy. Don't forget to take it when you go.' Then he reached into his pocket, handed each of them a small envelope. 'Those are MTN sim cards for your phones. They're already charged, so you should have plenty to last, unless you play too much Candy Crush.'

Daisy raised her eyes to the ceiling. 'Now who's being insulting? I might play too much Grand Theft Auto though.'

He shook his head. 'One day I just might get the better of you.'

'Not in my lifetime. Anyhow, thank you, Anton. And I know it's a lot to ask, but we wanted to beg two other favours of you. Get us going on the hunt for Celia, if you like.'

'I told you on Whatsapp, Daisy... any goddamn thing I can do to help sort this shit out.'

Aidan took over. 'We realise it's not easy, but we need a few names... we were told the man who bought Celia three years ago was a high-ranking military man, but there never was a name. We kind of need a short list, if you see what I mean. A starting point, I suppose.'

Anton nodded his bushy head. 'I can make a list of names, but it ain't gonna be easy to work out which one's keeping her. You must know what it's like being high-end military here. Kinda untouchable, a bit like the president.'

It was Daisy's turn to nod her head, a little sadly. 'We realise that, Anton. But we've got to try, and we've got to start somewhere.'

'Sure, Petal. You got it. And I'll help you sift through them with what little I know. But I'm due back in Nairobi tomorrow, so it might have to be from a distance. You said there was two things?'

Daisy brought him up to speed with what had happened at the airport, reached into her pocket and handed him the note the dying man had thrust into her hand. It didn't say much...

Ssebina Joseph. Jinja Barracks, 1964

'The man who died at my feet was Michael Ssebina. Going by the date on the note, it would seem to indicate he was maybe Joseph's son, or maybe a relative.'

Anton nodded slowly. 'Jinja Barracks in nineteen sixty-four rings a vague bell, but right now it's too far in the distance to hear it properly. When I get back to Nairobi tomorrow I'll trawl the embassy archives and look into it, see if I can shed any light.'

'Thanks, Anton. We'll do the same from here. Seems there's more than one mystery to solve now.'

'Geez, Daisy. How do you do it?'

'I don't. It just seems to do it to me.'

They spent a little time reminiscing over cocktails, and then Anton took his leave. He was invited to dinner, but couldn't stay. He'd built himself a house on the tiny island, and had to go shut it down, make sure Enid was safely on her way to her sister's, and then take the short cruise to

Entebbe harbour in his boat, to catch the night flight to Nairobi.

As he left he nodded to the bag of swimwear. 'Just be careful if you swim in that pool, Daisy. The water in this part of the world can be a little unpredictable, if you see what I mean?'

'I understand, Anton. If you won't stay for dinner, then let me offer our grateful thanks right now. We'll talk tomorrow. Safe journey, my friend.'

He shook Aidan's hand and embraced both the women, and was gone. Daisy picked up the bag, as Sarah whispered, 'What was he talking about, *unpredictable waters*?'

'Later, dear,' Daisy hissed, heading to the elevators. 'Let's dump this in the room first, and then we'll grab dinner.'

Daisy threw the sports bag onto the bed, but Sarah was the first to quickly unzip it. She pulled out a few costumes and towels. 'It is swimwear!'

'Anton is not a liar, Sarah. Not to those he likes, anyway.'

'But... *oh...*'

She reached deeper into the bag, and pulled out something he hadn't said was there.

Daisy grinned. 'Ah, an RPKS-74. Good man.'

'What? *A what?*'

'Dear, don't get too excited. It's just a Russian version of an automatic rifle. The 'S' bit means it's folding stock, so it would fit into the bag...'

'Sod folding stock... what the hell are you intending doing with it?'

'Just for protection, dear.'

Aidan peered over, but didn't look too surprised. 'Perhaps not the best idea, dear... shooting someone on foreign soil might be bad for our health.'

'Dip, I'm not intending actually *shooting* anyone. Maybe a gorilla or two, though... in the mist.'

'Very funny.'

'Glad you can still tell when I'm joking, dear.'

Sarah didn't look at all amused. 'Daisy? You're making me nervous now. No wonder you didn't tell me about Anton.'

'Sarah dear, it really is just about protecting ourselves, if things go wrong.'

'Now I'm even more nervous.'

'Anton is a bit of a collector, that's all. It's just a lend.'

'A *gun* collector?'

'Well, anything that goes bang really. He tells me his house on the island has a fine collection of Cold War devices.'

'*Devices?*'

'You know what I mean.' Daisy picked up the gun, unfolded the stock. 'This is one of the shipment of arms he and me stopped from getting from Kenya to Russia. I doubt it's been fired since. He likes to sneak away mementos.'

'Mementos? Of what?'

'Shall we go to dinner, dear? I'm starving!'

Chapter 5

In the white dining room with its elaborate gold chandeliers hanging from the ornate ceiling, they ate large meals which had a distinctive Indian flavour, and then Daisy ordered ice cream desserts for her and Sarah. Aidan declined, said he was full, and ready to spray himself with mosquito repellent and hit the bed. Daisy kissed him on the cheek, said she'd be up soon, and watched him go. Then she turned back to Sarah.

'Ok, you can ask me now.'

'Ask you what?'

'What you've been itching to ask ever since Anton left.'

'It's none of my business.'

'Don't you want to know?'

'Well of course I do.'

'Then stop pretending it's none of your business, and I'll tell you the story.'

'Oh, go on then.'

'Anton was the one who… stole my cherry.'

Sarah spluttered on a sip of wine she was just taking. As a fine mist sprayed out across the table, she let out a giggle and then covered her mouth with a hand in a slightly embarrassed way.

'Sorry… *seriously*?'

'What?'

'Um… I've never heard it put so… fruitfully before.'

'Just trying to keep the emotion out of it… give you the nutshell version, if you like.'

'Oh, no way. If Anton cracked your nut, I want all the gory details.'

'So now we're going from fruit to nuts?'

'Stop procrastinating. Just give me the juicy bits... sorry.'

'If you're sure.'

'You want me to get the juicer out?'

'Ok, if it stops the bad jokes. It was almost forty years ago, and it only lasted four weeks.'

'Wait... does Aidan know?'

'Course he does. We have no secrets. And it was a few years before I met him... well, before I saved his life, actually.'

'Oh wow... two juicy stories.' Sarah shook her head, but managed to grin at the same time. 'Sorry, must be the wine. Going a bit nuts here.'

It was Daisy's turn to shake her head. 'You really are in the wrong job, Officer Lowry. Then again, I can see it on the billboards... Sarah Lowry, the stand-up copper comedienne.'

'Ok, I'll shut up now. Chomping at the bit here...'

Daisy took a big gulp of her wine. 'It was a joint operation between the British Secret Intelligence Service and the CIA. Right in the middle of the cold war, we'd got intelligence that arms deals were going down on the Kenyan coast, for weapons that eventually found their way to Russia.'

'So you *were* a secret agent then, Jamie?'

'I guess I was. But this particular mission was like most of them outside of Hollywood movies... observation and information gathering. At least it was supposed to be.'

'So it got all Hollywood? But hang on... how old were you then?'

'I thought you were going to shut up?'

'Just answer the question.'

'Yes, Officer. I was thirty-two. Anton was ten years younger, a raw CIA recruit.'

45

'So you… lost your cherry at *thirty-two*?'

Daisy looked down to her hands, a smile on her face. 'Sarah, back then women weren't quite so keen to lose their virginity while they were teenagers. But I suppose the main reason was because of my job. Doing what I chose to do wasn't just a career, it was a way of life. A life that tended to put you off getting romantically involved, because any relationship was unlikely to last. Don't believe everything you see in the movies.'

'That's so sad. But Aidan… he must have somehow broken that cycle?'

'Yes he did. And it's also why we had Celia relatively late in life. But that's another story for another day. You want to hear about Anton or not?'

'I'm zipping it now, promise.'

'Hmm… we knew they had to be shipping the arms from somewhere near Mombasa, but not exactly where. Teams of two were staking out a few likely deserted beach-front locations. Anton and me were one of those pairs.'

'Wow… so you lost your cherry on a tropical beach in the African moonlight?'

'What happened to zipping it?'

'Sorry.'

'I was quite pretty then, and… well, starting to think saving it for marriage wasn't all my mother told me it was. Anton was full of beany enthusiasm, handsome, and a lot less hairy than he is now. And I guess being alone on a deserted beach on a warm, beautiful night, contributed to the ambience.'

'So who made the first move?'

Daisy closed her eyes, an action misinterpreted by Sarah. 'Sorry… shutting up for real now.'

46

But Daisy had closed her eyes as she recalled what was clearly a special moment. She spoke quietly, like she was living through it right there and then.

'We'd spent four hours watching nothing, then suddenly three men slipped out of the trees and stood on the beach, waiting for an open boat to arrive. When it did, they dragged it into the trees a couple of hundred yards from us, and disappeared. All went quiet. We'd taken photos of what had gone down, as per our instructions, and then got on the radio and reported it to the operation controllers.

'Their opinion was the boat wasn't going to be loaded and leave until the next night, so we were told to stand down and go get some sleep. But it was such a lovely, warm night...

'We should sleep here, Daisy flower. Under the stars, no one for miles, falling asleep with the sound of the waves crashing on a tropical beach.'

'You sound like a holiday brochure.'

Anton stretched out on the golden sand, just inside the tree line, his hands behind his head. 'You complaining?'

'It's tempting.'

She lay flat next to him, enjoying the feel of the soft warm sand moulding to her shape. He leant up on one elbow, spoke with a grin on his face. 'But?'

'But you might have your wicked way with me.'

'It takes two, where I come from.'

'That's what I'm afraid of.'

'So you're afraid you might *want* me to have my wicked way?'

'Maybe,' she whispered. 'I'm still... a bit lacking in experience in that field. Our jobs, and this cold war, you know...'

47

He caressed her face with a gentle finger. 'So I might be the one to deflower you, Daisy?'

'So now you're trying to be funny?'

He let out a little chuckle, and then kissed her softly. 'I ain't offering you my hand in marriage. I feel the same as you about this goddamn world we move in. But it doesn't mean we can't enjoy the moment, and look on it as just that.'

Daisy didn't speak for a minute, gazing into the eyes that never left hers. Then she lifted her top over her head, swallowed hard, and smiled. 'Just be gentle with me, Anton...'

Chapter 6

Sarah was a sitting statue, the wineglass she'd forgotten all about frozen in her hand. Finally she found her voice. 'Wow... now that *is* the stuff of movies.'

Daisy smiled, forcing her mind back to the there-and-then. 'I suppose it was. And he *was* gentle. He wasn't that experienced himself, but somehow we made... made a beautiful, unforgettable moment. But it wasn't the only memorable moment that night.'

'What happened?'

'Two hours later, he saved my life.'

'I'm still all ears.'

'I must have fallen asleep, the kind of blissful, satisfied sleep that cocoons you without you realising it. I didn't know how long I'd been away with the fairies, but then he nudged me in the ribs...

'Daisy, wake up. There's someone here.'

Thrust cruelly back to harsh reality, she could hear muffled voices a hundred yards away. Anton was already on his knees, peering through the trees to try and see something in the moonlight. Then, they both saw something.

The small boat which had arrived a few hours earlier has been pulled out of the trees onto the beach. It was high tide, and the ocean had risen to leave just a thin strip of beach. Right next to the gentle waves, the boat was already being loaded with wooden crates.

Anton was already on the radio, communicating the unexpected development to control. The voice on the other end sounded a little panic-stricken. *'Stay where you are. We're sending people, but it'll be a short while before they get there.'*

Anton glanced to Daisy, a real fear in his eyes. 'A short while will be too late. Five minutes and that boat will be gone.'

'There are four men. What can we do without backup?'

'Dunno... but we've got to do something. Grab your gun.'

'Anton, that's not really...'

Daisy stopped the sentence dead. Anton wasn't there to hear it. *'Oh, for crying out loud...'*

She ran from their hideaway, thirty feet behind Anton. He was already screaming at the men, who looked a little surprised someone with a gun in his hand was heading straight for them.

They didn't look surprised for long. Gun-runners who knew their stuff, the air was suddenly alive with the flash of gunfire. Anton fired back, hit one of them. Daisy fired too, killed another.

But then the two remaining bad guys made a calculated move. They dropped behind the crates on the boat, knowing their do-or-die action would either result in victory or, if a bullet hit the right crate, blow everyone to kingdom come.

Anton hesitated, all too aware of the volatile situation. In that moment one of the bad guys fired, and a bullet slammed into his leg. He crumpled to the ground. Daisy screamed, ran to him and dropped down beside him.

'It's just my leg... get clear, before...'

She glanced round to the boat. Both the men had sensed victory, and were heading towards them. Daisy fired, hit one of the men. The other fired back as he dropped to one knee, but missed. Daisy tried to fire again. The handgun was spent. She screamed out in frustration, threw the gun to the sand in disgust.

It maybe wasn't the best move ever. The bad guy saw her action, and realised she was helpless. Slowly, surely, he walked towards them, the semi-automatic raised to his shoulder.

'Ok, you win. Just go and leave us be,' Daisy cried, knowing he could never just go and leave them alive.

He confirmed that. A sneer of anticipation on his face, he answered in a foreign accent. 'You know I cannot go, not when there are people alive who can ruin everything.'

He lifted his weapon, a moment away from firing. But Anton wasn't quite finished.

'Times up, sucker...' he growled. Flat on the ground, he fired a bullet into the man, who crumpled onto the sand, dead.

Daisy dropped to the ground beside him, just as they heard a friendly shout from somewhere in the trees. The backup had arrived, just like the cops in a disaster movie when the heroes had already saved the day.

Daisy helped Anton sit up. Blood was seeping from his leg wound, but she could see he would be alright. 'You just saved my life, rookie,' she smiled. 'In more than one way.'

He grinned, and then looked ruefully at the handgun he was still holding. 'That's as maybe, Petal. But that was my last bullet...'

Sarah's jaw dropped open. 'Oh my god... so you're here today because of one tiny bullet.'

Daisy shook her head ruefully. 'I guess so.'

'So Anton made beautiful love to you, and then saved your life. Most people would be together forever after that.'

Daisy looked down to her lap again. 'We weren't most people, Sarah. We were in Kenya for another four weeks, during which time we... um... enjoyed each other's company a few more times. One of the bad guys I shot wasn't dead, and when the CIA leaned on him in hospital, he caved. Just before the mission ended, they broke the ring and arrested everyone connected.'

'Go you guys. But I still don't understand... you two seemed like a match made in heaven.'

'In a way we were. But there never was a future, and we both knew it. Separate careers in Intelligence beckoned, and we knew when the mission was called as complete, it was unlikely we would ever work together again.' She let out a deep sigh. 'But the final goodbye never did happen.'

'How so?'

'Referring to famous movies again, have you ever seen *Love is a Many Splendored Thing?*'

'Oh wow... um... William Holden, Jennifer Jones... the famous final scene on the hillside?'

Daisy nodded. 'Yes. That was kind of my scene. Not quite the same, but at the time it felt like it.'

'Please tell me,' Sarah begged, wiping a tear from her eye.

'We had a tree on a hilltop too. We'd decided it was best to keep our relationship a secret, for obvious reasons. We'd met a few times on that hill, just above Mombasa. Then my boss told me I'd be going home in a couple of days, so Anton and me arranged to meet one last time, by the tree on the hill. Just like the movie, he never turned up. I waited an age, even though I thought I saw him coming once, but it was someone else.'

Sarah sniffed back the tears. 'Why? Why didn't he come?'

'I flew back to the UK thinking he'd chickened out on a final goodbye. It was a few days later when he contacted me, said they'd virtually bundled him onto a flight back to America that day, and at the time we'd arranged to meet he was actually flying over me. He'd had no way to let me know.'

'Oh hell, that's so sad. You never saw each other again?'

Daisy shook her head. 'No. We kept in touch, sent Christmas cards and all that. But when Aidan came along, he kind of took all my attention. Anton fell in love with Africa, and a few years later got a posting, and he's been here ever since, growing hair and beards.'

'And was it... a many splendored thing, I mean?'

Daisy took a moment to answer. 'For those four weeks, I guess it was. But a bit like a holiday romance, we made precious memories too special to forget. It was hard for a while, but then Aidan came into my life, and made me realise what really mattered.'

Sarah wiped her eyes, took a big gulp of the wine. 'It's a beautiful, bitter-sweet story, Daisy. Thank you for trusting me enough to tell me.'

'Welcome to the club of those who know the truth, Sarah. You're only the fourth member!'

Chapter 7

A rather late breakfast was taken in the dining room, just before the staff cleared everything away. Back in the room, Aidan got straight on the laptop. Within twenty minutes he'd found something interesting, called the others over.

'Look... Jinja Barracks, nineteen-sixty-four. According to the newspaper archives, there was a bit of an event. Seems Ugandan troops mutinied, went on strike over pay and conditions, including the fact the British were still calling the military shots after independence.'

Sarah, peering at the screen over his shoulder, shook her head. 'So the then prime minister, Milton Obote, did the worst thing he could and asked the British to help quell the mutiny.'

Daisy, also reading the archive, let out a mirthless chuckle. 'So the British sent troops from Kenya, who managed to quell the unrest by doing one of the very things they were complaining about.'

Aidan nodded. 'Yes, British troops getting the local troops to surrender by British force.'

Daisy narrowed her eyes. 'It doesn't say anything about deaths or injuries though. It mentions a peaceful solution. Do you think that's what our mysterious note refers to?'

Aidan was still nodding. 'It has to be, it's just too much of a coincidence. Maybe something happened in those few days that wasn't common knowledge?'

'It seems a likely scenario. Keep trawling dear, see what more you can find out.'

Aidan kept trawling, but in the archives he could get access to, there was little new information. Then he switched to attempting to compose a list of high-ranking military officials, but didn't have a lot of luck there either. He managed to compile a list of four well-known names, but going any further would require access he didn't have.

Then, just before lunch, Daisy's phone rang. It was Anton. She flicked it to speaker.

'Hey, Flower. Making my way through the official archives now. Still early days, but I might have come across something related to Jinja Barracks in nineteen-sixty-four.'

'The Ugandan troop mutiny?'

He laughed. *'Guess you're already doing your own discovering then.'*

'We are, but there's nothing *that* interesting in the newspaper archives to tell the kind of story we need to get excited about.'

'No, there likely wouldn't be in the newspapers of the time. But I've found something that might get you juiced up.'

'Bad choice of phrase, Anton. But go on...'

'Sorry. But what you won't know, because it was hushed up, is that someone died.'

'Ok, but the papers said no one was killed or badly injured.'

'That's not what I mean, Daisy. From what I've discovered so far, it seems that during the unrest, a British army captain was murdered.'

'Ah, now it's getting interesting.'

'Thought you might say that. Still delving, so I'll call you with more later. And I'll let you have a list of names that might help you locate Celia.'

'Thanks, Anton. You're a star.'

Daisy killed the call, and looked at Aidan and Sarah. 'Now we might have a better reason why a dying man handed me a note.'

Just after lunch the house phone buzzed. Daisy answered it. The soft tones of the receptionist didn't do much to calm the sudden nerves.

'Mrs. Henderson, the police are here to see you. Shall I send them up?'

Daisy thought quickly. Regardless of why they'd come, there was something in the room that not many hotel rooms were supposed to have. 'No, we'll come down. Ask them to wait for us in the lobby.'

As they stepped from the elevator, three officers were waiting for them in the lobby area. One of them looked very high-ranking, and not the kind of man you'd want to mess with. Daisy marched up to him with a confidence she wasn't feeling, and smiled warmly.

'I'm Daisy Henderson. This is my husband Aidan, and our good friend Sarah.'

He removed his hat, and greeted them all. The light-khaki shirt was adorned with big black epaulettes, and official-looking badges that told her she needed to be very careful with her words. Then he introduced himself, and confirmed her worst fears.

'Good afternoon, Mrs. Henderson. I am Martin Osambu, Inspector General of Ugandan police. Pleased to make your acquaintance.'

Daisy swallowed hard. The biggest police gun of all had found it necessary to pay them a visit. 'I am honoured, sir.'

'Trust me, Mrs. Henderson, I would much rather be playing a round on Kololo golf course right now. But I wished to see how you were fairing, after your... unpleasant arrival to our wonderful country yesterday.'

Daisy bit her lip. Almost ready to retort that there had to be other reasons why he was there, she smiled sweetly instead. 'We are fine, thank you. No lasting effects, but we are concerned about the poor man who died. Is there any news on the cause of death?'

He hesitated, seemed reluctant to pass on sensitive information to a muzungu, especially one who he'd felt it necessary to meet in person. 'It is a rare and highly unfortunate occurrence in this peaceful country, but I should tell you he was... um, poisoned.'

'Poisoned?' cried Sarah. 'How? What with?'

'Snake venom. It would appear he was bitten by a Bitis Gabonica. Its common name is a Gaboon viper.'

Sarah turned away, looking a little green around the edges. Aidan frowned. 'A Gaboon viper, in this part of Uganda?'

'It is strange, I agree. They are found mostly in forests. It would not be incorrect to assume the venom was collected and administered deliberately. But you must not concern yourselves with this matter. We are conducting a thorough investigation. However I need to ask, are you in possession of a phial containing snake venom, Mrs. Henderson?'

'Oh come, Inspector General. Even if I had time to go and collect snake venom before I left the airport, I am sure such poison takes a little time to kill. The poor man was dead two minutes after he first saw me. Check out our passport stamps if you don't believe me.'

'I am sure that will not be necessary, Mrs. Henderson. You are all valued and important visitors to our peaceful country. I can only apologise that your visit here began in such terrible circumstances.'

'And we are deeply grateful for your concern, sir. May we respectfully ask you keep us informed of your investigations? That poor man...'

He lifted his captain's hat to his head, forced a smile to crease his craggy face. 'As long as you and the members of your party are coping with the ordeal, I shall take my leave. Please do not hesitate to contact one of my officers if you need anything. I bid you good day.'

He spun on his heels and marched away across the vastness of the ground floor, followed by his silent entourage of two.

'Enjoy the golf!' Daisy called out.

He lifted an arm to acknowledge her parting shot. She watched until he was out of sight, and then shook her head.

'What total bullshit.'

Chapter 8

Daisy and Aidan marched Sarah into the hotel bar, forced a Baileys down her. She still looked a little green.

'*Snake venom?* I think I'd rather hang.'

'No you wouldn't.'

'How would you know?'

Daisy wrapped a comforting arm around her shoulders. 'Well, I don't. Quite honestly both ways are barbaric, but at least it's told us a new fact.'

'That poor man knew something,' Aidan offered.

'For sure. Apart from the fact the law enforcement elite effectively made it clear they were keeping an eye on us, a British army captain was murdered years ago. For whatever reason it was hushed up, and his son, or whoever he was, discovered something that got him murdered to keep him quiet.'

'But all these years later?'

'That's the puzzling thing. But we'll have to rely on Anton to get more facts, because little us aren't going to unearth them ourselves, not now.'

Aidan agreed. 'I'll get back on the laptop, but I doubt I'll find anything else useful. The troops were sent from Nairobi, and there's still a British army training ground there. As Anton is based in Nairobi, maybe he'll have more luck discovering something from home base, as it were.'

Daisy looked into Sarah's eyes. 'You feeling better now?'

'Another Baileys might help.'

'Coming up. Then we'll get back to the room, let Aidan do his stuff. Hopefully Anton will call again later.'

Daisy and Sarah were sitting on the balcony watching the sun head to the city skyline when Anton's call came an hour later. She flicked it straight to speaker, as Aidan joined them.

'The plot thickens, guys. Still not got so much, but what I have found makes bigger waves. The captain who was murdered was Richard Mackenzie, who was based in Kenya but sent to Jinja to quell the mutiny. But his wife, also in the army, was based at Jinja. Seems she was having an affair with a young Ugandan private, who took his opportunity to murder the captain while he was at the barracks by throwing a grenade into his hut. He was arrested, and jailed for life. And life means life for a crime like that in these here parts.'

Straightaway, Daisy was putting two and two together. 'Is the private still alive, Anton?'

'Yes. He's seventy-four now. He admitted the murder, saying he wanted the captain's wife for himself. So there wasn't much of an investigation. Cut and dried seems to be the theme.'

'I still can't see a connection to our dead man, Anton.'

'You might when I tell you the private's name. It was Ssebina Joseph.'

Daisy let out a deep sigh. 'Yes, the plot does thicken.'

'For sure. And when I tell you the private's girlfriend, who married him in prison, became pregnant just before the night of the murder, that might fit a peg or two into holes.'

'She bore a son… Michael. He'd be fifty-six.'

'Was fifty-six,' Aidan corrected.

'You getting the picture now?' said Anton.

'Oh yeah. Somehow Michael discovered a clue about his father's crime which those involved didn't want to be made public. He paid with his life.'

60

Sarah was fitting a peg into another hole. 'He was catching a flight to Nairobi, where the British army base was then, and still is. Do you think he was going to see if someone there could shed any more light on whatever he'd discovered?'

Daisy and Aidan both nodded. 'That makes a lot of sense,' said Aidan. 'But someone who wanted secrets to remain secret found out, and stopped him in his tracks.'

He glanced to Daisy, and saw the narrow-eyed look he'd come to know so well. Then she spoke, in the tone he also knew well.

'Yes, for sure. But they haven't stopped *us* yet.'

Anton promised to keep digging, and told Daisy he'd got a list of high-ranking military names he was going to text to her, which might help start the search for Celia. She killed the call, looked up and smiled, but said nothing.

Aidan groaned to himself, but didn't speak either. It was already a given Daisy wouldn't stop until they'd found their daughter. But now he also knew she wasn't going to stop until she'd discovered what was so important to the total stranger who had died at her feet.

Chapter 9

Anton Kowalski stepped from the taxi into the heavy rain of a very wet Kenyan morning. He shook his head, sending a catherine-wheel of spray from the wide-brimmed hat protecting his head.

He splashed his way across the concrete forecourt of the BATUK base, and into the main administration building, where a young female private greeted him with a slightly strange look. He introduced himself, flashed his US embassy credentials, and explained he had a meeting with the camp commander.

She led him along a stark corridor, and into a more pleasantly-furnished room. A man in British army uniform stood up from behind an elegant mahogany desk, held out a hand.

'Good morning. Mr. Kowalski. I am Major Adam Winterton. Pleased to make your acquaintance.'

Anton took the hand, and then the seat indicated to him by the major. His moustached face frowned curiously. 'I will confess, Mr. Kowalski, I am a little curious as to why the American Embassy is interested in an incident that happened many years ago, and actually didn't involve any American personnel.'

Anton groaned inwardly. It was always going to be the first question asked, and he didn't have an officially-acceptable reason why the embassy was involved. 'Please, call me Anton, major. The truth is, this started out as a favour for some British friends, but is turning into what might be a more serious matter.'

The major raised his eyebrows. 'I hope you are not telling me you suspect British troops were in some way involved in... dubious exploits?'

Anton let out another internal groan. That was the second awkward question he'd anticipated, which didn't have a reassuring answer. 'At this stage I can't give you any guarantees. Until we have investigated further, we're not sure who was involved. It's possibly not anything to do with British personnel, but we can't yet be sure. Which is where my visit today comes in, and the hope your army records can shed more light on what happened.'

The major shook his head, reached for a file sitting on the desk. 'I will do what I can, but it's not much, I'm afraid. After your call yesterday I delved into the distant archives, found a report made by the army investigators at the time, but as you can see, it's not exactly extensive. From what I can tell it was an open and shut case.'

He handed Anton the file. The document inside was a little thin, to say the least. Just one sheet of washed-out paper told him pretty much what he already knew, apart from one fact. He scanned through it, which took all of a minute, and then lifted his eyes to the major.

'It says there were reports of *two* explosions? The private was recorded as throwing one grenade into the hut.'

'Yes. The investigators apparently decided there was already a second grenade in the hut, possibly simply being stored there. The grenade thrown into the hut likely ignited the second device, which exploded a second later.'

'A little strange though, don't you think, major? A single grenade, stored in the captain's hut?'

'Perhaps. Who knows what the captain was thinking back then? He'd just been thrust into the middle of a Ugandan troop rebellion, sent into a volatile situation in a place he was not so familiar with. Maybe it was something to do with having a comfort blanket, making him feel a little more secure?'

'Maybe. Guess we'll never know.'

'Indeed. And as you will be aware, there's no one still here who could shed a light on what happened fifty-seven years ago. Although...'

'Major?'

'It's just occurred to me. There's one man here who could well have been there way back.'

'Seriously?'

The major nodded. 'We'll have to ask him, but it's a possibility. This site here at Kifali is virtually the same place the original barracks was built, from where the troops were sent to quell the mutiny. The catering has always been done by army personnel, but with help from the local civilian population. One old boy has been here forever... part of the furniture, you might say. Jacob should have retired years ago but he didn't want to, and no one had the heart to ask him to go. Nowadays he potters around doing odd catering jobs, but he seems quite happy. He's a good old stick, and it's very likely he was here in sixty-four.'

'Is he here now? Could I meet him?'

'Quite honestly he's here every day. But he's well into his eighties, so I'm not sure his memory will be so sharp now.'

'Got to be worth finding out though, hey major?'

Chapter 10

Anton and the major found Jacob sitting on a slab of stone under an open shelter attached to the side of the catering hut. Peeling potatoes with a small knife that looked almost as old as he was, he looked up as they walked over, and narrowed his eyes suspiciously.

The major gave him a deliberately wide smile. 'Good morning, Jacob. How are you today?'

He cast a gaze over the unusual appearance of one of his visitors, answered in a deep, husky voice. 'Good, as I always is, boss. I done something wrong?'

'No, not at all, Jacob. But you might be able to help us with something. This is Anton, from the American embassy. He'd like to talk with you, if you agree?'

Jacob looked Anton over again. 'A cowboy gunslinger, wants to talk to *me?*'

Anton guffawed. 'That's a new one, Jacob. Kinda like it. But no guns... not in Kenya anyways.' He sat down next to the old Kenyan man, offered him a cigar, which Jacob took. Major Winterton left them to it, headed back to the admin building.

Jacob looked at the cigar between his fingers. 'A New Cuba Connecticut? What I done to deserve this?'

Anton lit him up, and then his own. 'I see you know your cigars, Jacob. Trust me, these are hard to come by in these here parts. But you could be worth your weight in gold, so that's why you deserve it. Might even leave you with another one.'

'How so?'

'I'm looking into an incident that happened a long time ago, at Jinja barracks in Uganda...'

'You talking 'bout the death of Captain Mackenzie?'

'I see you're no fool, Jacob.'

'I ain't no fool... but I wasn't there, sir.'

'No I realise that, but you were here when the troops got back a few days later?'

Jacob's eyes glazed over. He sucked a long draw on the cigar, took a moment to answer. 'It was a bad doo, for them all. Neither the Scots Guards or the Staffordshire Regiment had lost a man for a long time, then they goes to quell a mutiny by supposedly friendly troops and a captain gets killed. It shook 'em up, for sure.'

'I guess the circumstances didn't help.'

'Sure. Captain Mackenzie's best friend got spooked more than most. He resigned his commission, and then I heard he went back to England a broken man.'

'His friend?'

Jacob nodded. 'William Rushmore. Hardly said a word to no one when he got back here, like he'd had his spirit ripped straight out of him. Then one day he was gone. The rest of 'em took weeks to get over the upset... an' all over a woman, from what I hear.'

'Yes it was, Jacob. But maybe not *exactly* what you heard. Thank you my friend, you have been a great help.'

Jacob smiled warmly. 'Ain't sure what I've done, cowboy. But it was good to meet you.'

Anton handed him another cigar, shook his hand, and headed back to the administration building.

'Jacob said something interesting. It might be something or nothing, but you may be able to help a little more, major.'

66

The camp commander handed Anton a cup of tea the orderly had just made. 'Whatever I can do. But I'm still not sure what.'

'Jacob said the dead captain had a good friend, William Rushmore, who took his death hard. Seems he resigned his commission, went back to the UK. Do you have records of ex officers, so we can find out if he's still alive?'

The commander sat down behind his desk, began pressing keys on the keypad. 'You think he had something to do with it?'

'No idea. But where women and love are concerned, I ain't ruling anything out.'

'If he'd been in the service for a while, he'd have some kind of army pension.'

Anton sat back, sipping his tea, wishing it was coffee, and waited while the major searched through the army database. Five minutes later, he lifted his eyebrows.

'Here it is... he's still alive, living in Halesworth, Suffolk. He's in his early eighties now, but more than that isn't in the records. That might help you though.'

Anton nodded, shook the major's hand. 'It don't mean a lot to me, but I know three people who might be grateful for the information. You and Jacob have been a great help, major.'

·

Chapter 11

'That one looks suspicious.'

Aidan glanced up from the list on the screen of twelve names Anton had provided them with, that he'd just transferred to the laptop. 'How can you possibly know that, dear?'

'I just do. Call it a gut feeling.'

'From a Ugandan name? Just how far does your gut reach?'

Sarah grinned. 'I might not have known you guys long, but you Aidan should know by now Daisy's gut needs to be taken seriously.'

'Oh, I take it seriously, especially after a Vindaloo… but picking one name from twelve on a gut feeling?'

Daisy glared at him. 'Well, just look at it. *Oyite Emmanuel*. Sounds like a man who can't be trusted to me.'

Aidan shook his head. 'I'll see what I can find out… about *all twelve*, ok?'

'If you insist, dear. But he's the one. Start with him.'

He groaned out the words. 'Yes dear.'

A simple lunch had just arrived in the room when Daisy's phone rang. Anton brought them up to speed with what he'd discovered.

'So this best friend is still alive. Halesworth, you say?' Daisy looked pointedly at Sarah.

'Yeah. Sounds like he might be able to shed a light, if he's still got all his marbles.'

'Typical. Halesworth is only a short drive from Norfolk, and we're on the other side of the world!' Again the eyes pierced into Sarah's.

'Sure you'll find a way, Petal. I've also found out Joseph Ssebina is serving his sentence in Makindye prison. That's a little closer to you... you can pretty much see it from where you are. If that bit of info is any use.'

'Oh, it just might be. Thanks, Anton.'

'Any luck with those names I sent over?'

'Yes. We know who it is.'

'What, already?'

Daisy caught Aidan's glance, saw the shake of his head. 'Well, I think I know. Call it a gut reaction.'

'Geez, again?'

'Don't you start.'

She heard a chuckle. 'Keep me in the loop.'

He ended the call. Then Daisy felt Sarah's glare. 'What?'

'Why did you keep looking at me like that?'

'You know very well why.'

Sarah threw her hands in the air. 'You want me to get Burrows involved.'

'Well, he's there and we're here.'

'He'll want to know what it's all about.'

'Tell him the truth. About the dead man anyway. Keep quiet about the rest of it. Just say there might have been a miscarriage of justice... he'll understand.'

'So this is your idea of taking me away from it all?'

Daisy walked over to Sarah and pulled her into a hug. 'I know. I'm sorry. I really didn't plan for someone to drop dead at my feet before we'd even left the airport.'

Sarah grinned. 'I suppose not. And it's so exciting!'

Aidan was shaking his head again, eating a sandwich as he trawled the internet. 'This *suspect* of yours, dear... he's a pretty high up bigwig, and judging by his photos, a formidable opponent who loves the power that goes with the position. The word untouchable springs to mind.'

Daisy peered at the screen. 'I told you he was the one.'

'I never said that!'

'Well, look at him. He looks exactly like the type of thug who would buy a pretty white girl.'

This time Aidan threw his eyes to the ceiling in despair. 'Dear, you're just slipping into the realms of hopeful fantasy.'

'You'll eat your words when I'm proved right.'

He buried his face in his hands. 'And how do you propose we prove you right, Mystic Meg?'

'We go and see him, of course. Where does he live?'

'Kololo. But...'

'There you go then... just across the way.'

'Now you're scaring me, Flower.'

'Kind of scaring myself too, if I'm honest. But first Sarah and me have a different visit to make.'

'We do?' said a wide-eyed Sarah.

'I take it you brought your badge?'

'Daisy... I am getting to know you enough to realise you'll use me in every possible way.'

'Dear, with the best possible intentions of course.'

'Of course.'

'Then first thing in the morning we'll pop to Makindye prison and say hello to Joseph.'

Aidan gasped. 'Just like that?'

Sarah shook her head. 'Not the legal representative and the police officer trick again?'

'It worked before. And we're playing it in a different country now.'

Aidan buried his face in his hands again. 'Daisy...'

'It'll be fine, Dip. And a word with the murderer will help a lot, don't you think?'

'You really will be the death of me.'

'You'll survive.'

'I take it you brought the wig?'

'Of course.'

'This is so exciting!'

Aidan stuffed the rest of his sandwich into his mouth, so it would be impossible to say any more argumentative words. Daisy grinned, took Sarah to one side. 'We need to get Burrows onside now. I didn't really want to involve him, but with this rather unexpected development he's the one perfectly placed to visit the other piece of this jigsaw, which just might help complete the picture.'

'He'll swear a lot.'

'But he'll do it.'

'Course he will. He's almost as bad as you for not being able to resist a mystery.'

'That's what I thought. You want to give him a call now?'

'Good a time as any, I suppose.'

'Ok. Then after that, sit down with Aidan and write him a mail with everything we know so far, so when he goes to see Mr. Rushmore he's got all the facts.'

'He'll tell me you're a pain in his butt.'

'Well, I suppose he's right on that one.'

Chapter 12

'It's a motorbike!'

'Yes dear. A boda-boda.'

'And I was worried about the plane ending up in Lake Victoria.'

'They're perfectly safe, dear. And registered, and legal. Well, mostly.'

'Not filling me with confidence here, Daisy.'

'Would I deliberately put you in danger, Sarah?'

'That's a subject we could discuss all day.'

'Kids. Never satisfied.'

Sarah climbed onto the rear seat behind the teenage driver, making sure she aimed a glare at Daisy before she did. Daisy straddled the second bike, called across to Sarah as the engines fired up. 'Don't worry, dear. It's only twenty minutes... well, ten, probably!'

'Still not filling me wi...'

The sentence wailed to a fade, as the bike sped away like it was on a Moto 3 grid.

As they weaved between the traffic and about a million other motorcycles, Daisy began to wonder if ten minutes was a bit of an exaggeration. Holding onto her briefcase like her life depended on it, the two drivers seemed to believe they were the kings of the road.

It might also have been a bit of a competition, to see which one of them could petrify their personal muzungu first.

It *was* just a ten minute roller coaster ride. As they raced up Makindye Hill, Daisy let out a sigh of relief. Sarah, just up ahead, didn't look like she was even physically capable of letting out a sigh, or anything else. Yet as they screeched to a stop in a cloud of dust outside the main entrance to the prison, she did actually manage to move, staggering away from the boda-boda like it was going to eat her for dinner.

She ripped off her helmet, thrust it into the hands of the grinning teenage rider, and strode over to Daisy in a bow-legged kind of way.

'Don't you ever do that to me again!'

'Sarah dear, we've still got to get back when we're done here.'

'Then I'll pay for a proper taxi.'

'No need, dear. Just thought you'd like to experience a little Ugandan street life.'

'So am I supposed to believe you actually enjoyed that?'

Daisy tapped her on the arm as she turned and headed for the prison. 'Let's just say we'll find a minibus for the trip home, if you'd rather.'

'How did you keep that wig on when you pulled your crash-helmet off, anyway?'

'It's amazing how versatile chewing gum is, dear.'

'Seriously?'

'Ok, I used Blu Tack. Happy now?'

They were sitting on steel chairs in the prison reception room, waiting for the suspicious Ugandan officer behind the desk to obtain clearance from someone higher up than himself, and make sure allowing civilian muzungus to visit a military prisoner wasn't going to get him into trouble.

Daisy had flashed the fake business card she'd used before, and Sarah had flashed the very real police badge she'd used unofficially before, back when they'd managed to get a visit with Roland Spence in Belmarsh prison.

That was the meeting which started the chain of events that had led to today's prison visit, even though the current visit had nothing to do with the original reason they were in Uganda.

Just everything to do with something which landed at Daisy's feet as soon as they arrived.

The reception officer walked back through the door from the rear office, smiled a little nervously. 'Mrs. Bundy, you may meet with the prisoner, for five minutes only. He is currently in the recreation yard; I will have him brought to an interview room.'

'No, thank you officer. If it is acceptable, can we meet with him in the yard?' Daisy smiled sweetly, hoping it would be acceptable. A private conversation in a quiet room with guards listening in could be much less private than it would be the open air.

'As you wish. But you will have an officer with you at all times.'

He led them through a maze of stark, white-painted corridors, and then finally pushed open a heavy door with latch bolts fastened all over it. The bright late-morning Ugandan sun made Daisy's eyes narrow as they were led across the open concreted space.

There were only ten or so inmates mooching around the recreation yard. The officer explained they only allowed a few prisoners at a time to have access to the outside world, staggering the half-hour allotments to try and avoid prison breaks.

Daisy narrowed her eyes for a different reason, as she took in their surroundings. It looked highly unlikely anyone would be insane enough to try to escape from the recreation yard, surrounded by fifteen-foot walls with barbed-wire tops, and crude guard-towers on both outside corners.

It reminded her of a German prisoner-of-war camp, and judging by the apparent age of the buildings, the place had very likely been there in the Second World War.

She shook her head. Half the people detained there had probably done nothing wrong by western standards. Joseph Ssebina *had* done something wrong, but it didn't alter the fact he'd spent his whole adult life confined in its grim surroundings.

The officer pointed to a small, white-haired man sitting on a crude wooden seat in one corner of the yard, reading a book. Then he nodded to the guard, and headed back to his reception desk.

Sarah looked sadly at Daisy, a slight mistiness in her eyes as the lonely and slightly-pathetic sight of the elderly man triggered unexpected emotions. Daisy nodded slowly, knowing exactly what she was feeling.

'Joseph, I'm Flora Bundy. This is Officer Sarah Lowry. We've come all the way from England to see you.'

He lifted his dull eyes from the book and shook his head, almost imperceptibly. A slight smile made the lines on his face a little deeper, but there was no mirth in it. The words were spoken slowly, quietly. 'Now why would you bother to do that? And why's you wearing that crazy wig?'

Daisy's hand inadvertently caressed one side of the long auburn locks. Slightly taken-aback, she glanced quickly to the guard, who was watching the other prisoners in a disinterested kind of way, and didn't seem to be listening to the giveaway conversation.

'Um… shall we walk a little?'

Joseph placed the book on the seat, and stood up like he really didn't want to. His demeanor was a little stooped, and he seemed to walk with difficulty. He was in his seventies after all, and life in an African prison wasn't exactly conducive to good health. Daisy steered them close to the wall, where there was a little cooler shade.

'Are you okay to walk, Joseph?'

'Sure. I just get a little stiff if I sit too long.'

'We don't have very much time, so I'll get straight to it. We wanted to visit you because some new facts have come to light about that night in nineteen-sixty-four.'

He stopped walking, looked at her incredulously, and then shook his head. 'What new facts? There ain't new facts. Situation was cut and dried.'

'Was it, Joseph?'

'Course it was. I threw that grenade into the captain's hut. No one else. I's guilty as charged, lady.'

Chapter 13

Daisy fixed her stare into the man who was giving nothing away. 'We realise you did it, Joseph. What we don't know is why.'

He shook his head again. 'You some kind of journalist? You ain't no brief, that's for sure.'

'I'm a real police officer though,' Sarah offered, not helping at all.

Daisy threw her a quick glare, and then put a hand on Joseph's slender shoulder. The guard was a few feet away, still looking like he's rather be sipping a beer somewhere else. She whispered. 'Ok, you got me sussed. I'm a... a private detective. But I'm on your side.'

'Then you is on a losing wicket there, honey.'

'I don't join losing teams, Joseph. So *why* did you do it?'

'You must know the facts, if you come all the way here. It was over a girl... I lost my head. I was seventeen, just joined the Ugandan Rifles. She... she rocked my boat, sent me crazy.'

'I don't believe that, Joseph.'

'Then you's crazy too. Them's the facts.'

Daisy sighed, deliberately loudly. 'Yes, we're aware of the party line. But we need the reality, Joseph.'

'I ain't got nothing more to say. Sorry you wasted your time.'

Sarah glared at him, and spat out the words angrily. 'So what about your girlfriend? Didn't she matter? She was pregnant at the time you were gallivanting with a captain's wife.'

Daisy opened her mouth to say something, but then decided to keep quiet. Suddenly aware of what Sarah was trying to do, she left her to her fake disgust. Joseph locked into her stare for a millisecond, but then looked away. Not soon enough for them both to notice the mistiness of pain in his eyes. He answered Sarah's accusations in a faint whisper.

'She... I didn't know she was carrying. She only told me... after.'

'And how did that make you feel?'

The mistiness turned into a tear, which Joseph wiped away with the back of his hand. 'How do you think I felt, muzungu?'

'I think however you felt, you knew you'd made the biggest mistake of your life. And I'm not referring to killing the captain.'

He ran a shaking hand across his shaved head. 'You... you leave Florence out of this, you hear me? Whatever you's up to, she ain't nothin' to do with it, ok?'

Daisy tried to smile reassuringly. 'It's ok, Joseph. Your wife is not part of this, I promise. But you married, so she must have still have believed in you.'

'We got special dispensation, coz she was with child. We married... here, in the prison.'

'So she never believed you were unfaithful?'

'She... it don't matter what she believed, ok? She's a crazy woman too.'

'So why did you marry her then?'

'It was my duty... she was carrying my child.'

Sarah stopped walking and stood in front of him, so he had to look at her. 'So you're pretty hot on *duty* then, Joseph?'

He stared at her for a few seconds, and then turned away and called out. 'Guard, this interview is over. Please show these people back to reception.'

The young guard looked a little bemused, but threw a questioning look to Daisy, who nodded. 'Yes, ok. We'll go now.'

They made their way back towards the heavy door in the concrete wall. Daisy had one more card to lay on the table, even though she was reluctant to play it. As they walked, she spoke quietly to Joseph. 'I'm sorry about the death of your son, Joseph. It must have been a shock for you.'

He hesitated for a second. 'He turned out a good man, somehow. Better than his father. They will not let me attend his funeral, and that is almost as hard to live with as his untimely death.'

'I'm so sorry.'

The guard knocked loudly on the door, and they heard the heavy bolts being drawn back. Joseph wiped away another tear.

'Michael came to visit me, sometimes. It was always a joy to see him. Watch him growing into a fine man. Having him taken away before me is wrong, especially by something as unexpected as a heart attack. It is hard for me and his mother to live with.'

'Heart att..?' Sarah's cry died away as Daisy glared at her to button it. She didn't utter another syllable until the main door to the prison slammed shut behind them, and they found themselves back on the dusty road. Then she repeated herself, completing the sentence this time.

'Heart attack?'

'Sorry about the glare, Sarah, but it's perhaps best not to shake the applecart too much. For now, anyway.'

'What the hell is going on?'

'A lot more than we understand right now.'

'They told that poor man his son died of a heart attack.'

79

'Yes, and we need to know why... not that the reasons are difficult to work out.'

'Someone high up doesn't want the slightest little wave to ripple the lake.'

Daisy turned to look at Sarah, saw her stroke away a tear with a finger. She put a consoling arm around her shoulder. 'Don't worry, dear. I'm more determined than ever to get to the bottom of this now.'

'Thank you, Daisy. That was a hard interview to get through. The poor man is petrified about something.'

Daisy nodded. 'I know. And I think what he's petrified about is the truth coming out, for whatever reason. Let's get back to the hotel. Burrows might have been to see William Rushmore by now, and be able to shed more light.'

'Ok. Just no motorbikes, *please?*'

Chapter 14

DCI Burrows put the phone down, and groaned to himself. He'd just been informed of a serious incident at the Kings Lynn docks, and knew he really should be there to oversee the police involvement.

He'd been looking forward to a nice drive in the countryside to Halesworth, even though it was little more than a favour for Daisy Morrow, his favourite pain in the butt. Halesworth wasn't that far from Kings Lynn, but it was far enough to make it a pleasant day out for him.

The unexpected call he'd received from Sarah Lowry late the previous afternoon had sounded serious. She'd virtually begged him to go and see William Rushmore, find out if he could shed any light on the puzzle. When he'd read the email that arrived an hour later, his puzzle-solving nature had been fired into overdrive, and he'd decided he had to make the trip to Suffolk the next morning.

For his own curiosity as much as anyone else's.

Once he'd located Rushmore's address on the police database, it had suddenly become more urgent. The man was living in a nursing home, and when he'd called to arrange the meet, had been told he was very near the end of his life. If he didn't talk with him very soon, it would be too late anyway.

Now a new case had been thrown at his doorstep, and by rights should take priority over the favour of a matter that strictly-speaking did not involve the UK police, or even a man who was suspected of any crime.

Rights were one thing though. Gut feelings and curiosity were another.

He shook his head, strode into the squad room, and found one of his detectives who didn't look like he had much to do. So he made his day, gave him point on the case at the docks.

Two hours later he was driving through the pretty and ancient market town of Halesworth, following the directions of his sat nav to the Shady Oaks Nursing Home. Ten minutes after that, he climbed out onto the elegant gravelled drive, and gazed up at the impressive facade of the four-storey Edwardian mansion that was once the family home of a local dignitary.

The receptionist asked him to wait, but it was only two minutes before he was greeted by an African nursing sister, who led him along an elegant wide walkway adorned with potted plants in big square floor-standing pots. She cautioned him as they walked.

'Please respect the fact William is at the end of his life, Inspector. If he has been involved in some kind of wrongdoing, you must appreciate he will not live long enough to serve any punishment you may wish to pursue through the law.'

'Oh, this is not a criminal matter, sister. We simply believe he may have information that could help with another case.'

'I am glad about that. By rights he should be in hospital, but his wish was to bow out in the nicer and more peaceful surroundings of this home. He still has his faculties, but I will admit he has seemed a little more uneasy in the last few weeks. It is like something is bothering him, perhaps because he knows the end of his life is close, and whatever it is needs to be resolved. He won't say anything to us though.'

Burrows smiled to the nurse who might have just hit the nail on the head. 'Perhaps he will talk with me, sister.'

William Rushmore didn't look at all well. Lying propped up on pillows in the bed in his elegantly-furnished private room, there seemed to be wires and tubes attached all over his body. He turned his head a little as Burrows walked into the room.

'Good morning, Inspector. Please tell me you have news for me.'

Burrows hesitated. The voice was hoarse, the words slightly breathless, but they were clear enough. And not the words he expected to hear. He pulled up a chair by the side of the bed, smiled warmly. 'That depends on what kind of news you were expecting, William.'

'Call me Will, please. I have final-stage lung cancer, Inspector, so the least you can do is grant me that wish.' He let out a little chuckle, which ended in a cough. 'I'm sorry. There is little time left, as you can probably see.'

'I'm sorry, Will. The news you speak of... is that news from here in the UK, or from Uganda?' he asked, fishing for a clue.

'I think you know the answer to that, Inspector, otherwise you wouldn't be here.'

'Indeed, Will.' Burrows pulled a small recorder from his pocket. 'I'd like to record our conversation. Just to save me missing anything, and writing it all down from memory. It that okay?'

Will nodded, and then rested his head back on the pillows, looking like he didn't have the strength to hold it up anymore. But there was a smile on his face. 'It is a huge relief to know Michael got the tape.'

83

Burrows opened his mouth to ask what tape he was referring to, but the desperately ill man coughed again, and it looked like it had sapped even more life from him. 'Shall I fetch someone?' he asked instead.

'No... there is nothing anyone can do for me. Tell me, has the tape been useful?'

Burrows thought quickly, rapidly putting two and two together and making a very definite four. He watched as the poor man tried to suck in grating breaths that were just as painful to witness, clearly in the last throes of his life. And he didn't have the heart to tell him the man he'd sent the tape to was dead, likely because of the tape itself.

'I have an officer in Uganda now, with two other people, who are reopening the case, Will.'

He looked like a great weight had suddenly been lifted. 'It has been a burden on me ever since that night, Inspector. Not the least because I failed in my duty to my best friend. It is something that has troubled my thoughts every day, and although I am ashamed to admit it, it is only my imminent death that has led me to become less of a coward.'

'I don't understand, Will. Why would you think you were a coward?'

William coughed again, and it looked for a moment he didn't have the strength to suck in any air. Then he managed to take a faltering breath. Burrows slipped the oxygen mask around his face. 'I really think I should call someone.'

William dropped the mask to his chin, spoke in a whisper. 'Please allow me to answer your question first, Inspector. Richard Mackenzie was a fine, honourable man. He lived his life through strong beliefs and principles. Which sadly in the end, was the reason he died.'

'Can you explain that, Will? I still don't see why you saw yourself as a coward.'

He swallowed hard, and it looked like even that was painful. 'Please, would you pass me some water? Even reaching out for the glass is becoming too much for me.'

Burrows held the glass to his lips, made sure he managed a couple of sips. He looked grateful, but then his eyes narrowed still further.

'Richard confided in me, Inspector. Begged me to do two things for him. I did the one thing I shouldn't have, and didn't do the thing I really should have.'

'You must have had your reasons. But why do you feel there was cowardice involved?'

Burrows felt the man's hand wrap feebly around his forearm. He glanced up to his pale face, saw tears in his eyes. They were tears of a different kind of pain.

He whispered a deathbed confession.

'Because I was the one who killed him, Inspector. Twice over, in a way.'

Chapter 15

For a moment Burrows couldn't answer. Whatever he'd anticipated from their conversation, a confession wasn't it.

'You're confusing me. It's my understanding it was a cut and dried case of who threw the grenade into the command hut.'

'Yes, I know. That was indeed never disputed. But it's also only a small part of the truth.'

'Now you've got my attention, Will. May I know the truth?'

He asked for another sip of water, which Burrows gave him. It seemed like it was getting visibly harder for him to swallow, but he looked determined to tell his story.

'You must understand Inspector, back then things were different. Richard was a principled man, brought up by his father who was also an army man, with what were considered old-fashioned values, even then. Some would call Richard overly prim and proper. When he married Mary, it raised a few eyebrows, including mine.'

'Why?'

'Let me be kind, and say she didn't possess Richard's principles. She was a very attractive woman, also in the army, and based at Jinja barracks. With Richard based in Nairobi, they didn't see much of each other. Which gave her plenty of freedom to... do her own thing, as it were.'

Burrows shook his head. 'I get the feeling you are being kinder to her than you really feel.'

'A year after Richard's death, back in England she committed suicide. She blamed herself, and never got over it. I will not speak too ill of the dead, Inspector.'

'From what I hear now, she wasn't the only one, Will. But she *was* the one having the affair with the Ugandan private that led to Mackenzie's death, after all.'

He shook his head slowly, closed his eyes again. 'You are partly right, Inspector. But it wasn't Joseph Ssebina she was having the affair with. It was someone else, a sergeant in the Ugandan Rifles.'

'But I was told...'

'Allow me to tell you more. A few days before the mutiny in Jinja, a friend based there told me Mary was seeing someone. It didn't surprise me, but I deliberated too long on telling Richard, partly because I knew he would refuse to believe me, partly because if he did accept the news, I knew what it would do to him. In his world, when you married, you committed yourself to your partner. Infidelity was unthinkable.'

'So what did you do?'

'I had finally decided to speak with him about it, but before I had chance we were rushed to Jinja to quell the mutiny. The next day, I didn't need to tell him.'

'Why?'

'He was reunited with his wife after six weeks in separate barracks. The first night after our arrival, they had dinner together. Over that meal, Mary told him the truth.'

'I see. I guess he didn't take it so well.'

'He was distraught. The following day he carried out his duties, and we quelled the Rifle's mutiny. By the time night fell, all was calm. But I could see he was desolate. For a principled man like him, the news his wife was having an affair with a Ugandan man was devastating.'

'Did he confide in you?'

William asked for more water. Burrows refilled the glass from the sink in the corner, and made sure he drank a little.

87

Somehow he looked weaker than ever, but at the same time, like a weight had been lifted. He spoke so quietly it was little more than a hoarse whisper.

'I went to the command hut to see if he would talk with me about it. He was sitting alone behind the desk, staring into space. I asked him to talk with me, but he didn't seem willing or able. He just asked me to fetch a grenade from the armoury, speaking in emotionless monotones.'

'That was a strange thing to say though.'

'Perhaps. But I knew deep down what was in his mind. I started to protest, but he grew angry and told me to do as he said. He was a rank or two above me, and friend or not, you didn't question orders. So I fetched the grenade, and spent the rest of my life wishing I hadn't.'

'But you didn't kill him, surely?'

William shook his head, a weak side to side movement that nevertheless emphasised his anguish. The gloss was back in his lifeless eyes. 'Didn't I? I could have refused his request.'

'I can't see that would have made a difference. He would have just fetched one himself.'

'I suppose so. But I should have refused, nevertheless.'

'So what happened next?'

'I got back to the hut ten minutes later. He was just taking a cassette out of his Dictaphone. Cassette tapes had just been invented, a new-fangled device that made recording easier. Richard was into the tech of the time. He handed the tape to me. There were tears in his eyes. Still he was speaking in monotones, like he was on autopilot. But I shall never forget his words.

'*Thank you for bringing me the grenade, Will. I have just recorded a message for my... my wife. Please give it to her tomorrow, when she returns to base. Now leave, please. I wish to be alone.'*

'Hell. What did you do?'

William was trying to blink away the tears, his arms unable to lift from the bedclothes. Burrows grabbed a tissue, dabbed them away. He gave him a weak smile of thanks.

'I refused to leave at first, but then Richard grew angry, and told me to take the tape and go, and that I had no business interfering in private matters. Still I refused to go, but then he pulled rank again, something he never did outside working hours, and virtually pushed me out of the door.'

'So you blame yourself, Will?'

'Of course I do. I should have fought harder to stop him doing what I knew he was going to do. And I should have refused to accept the tape. But... but it was his last wish. I didn't know what to do. I stumbled away from the hut with the tape in my hand, dropped onto my bunk in the sergeant's quarters, a million terrible thoughts running through my head.'

'You still didn't actually kill him, Will.'

'Perhaps I didn't literally throw the grenade that the records say ended his life. But I did take him the grenade that *actually* killed him.'

Chapter 16

'I don't understand, Will. The records state that Joseph Ssebina threw a grenade into the hut.'

'Yes, he did. That was never in dispute. But it wasn't the actual grenade that killed him.'

'Tell me how you know that.'

Will coughed again, and it seemed to rip away a little more of his life. 'Forgive me, Inspector. The pain in my chest is becoming a bit too much to cope with.' Burrows wrapped a hand around his. It felt cold, and when he spoke, the words were only just discernible.

'I decided I must tackle Richard again, stop him doing what I knew he intended. But I had only just walked through the door from the sergeant's quarters when I saw the command hut explode, fifty feet away from me. The young Ugandan recruit was just running away. Myself and two others apprehended him. He admitted to throwing the grenade into the hut, right there and then, and in addition, the two other men had seen him do it.'

'So it appears to be open and shut.'

'But there were *two* explosions, Inspector. One second apart. I did not know at the time, but I found out which grenade had actually killed Richard a few days later.'

'How?'

'I needed to know for sure. The Ugandan police had not been that thorough. It was, as you said, an open and shut case. But only I suspected the truth. Richard had confided in me, no one else. The next day we returned to Nairobi, and the captain's body was taken back with us. The Scots Guard medics examined what was left of it, but they couldn't offer a reasonable explanation of what they found, so the matter was closed.'

'What they found?'

'What little was left of Richard's body told a different story, but only to me. I worked in the administration building at the Kahawa barracks in Kenya. It was therefore easy for me to take the medical report, which had already been archived. His remains indicated he was killed by a grenade exploding right next to his body. He'd been sitting behind his desk, which was not in a direct line from the door. A grenade thrown through the door, which witnesses saw Joseph do, could not have got close enough to cause such devastating injuries.'

'So you are saying the captain actually killed himself?'

'It is a virtual certainty the grenade I gave him was in his hands when he pulled the pin. Now do you understand how I killed him, Inspector?'

Burrows ran a hand across his mouth. In one way he could see where Will was coming from, but he was still being unfair to himself. A principled man like Richard Mackenzie would have taken his life anyway, with or without his help.

'I understand how you feel, Will. But I doubt you would have stopped him, from what you tell me of his character. Ultimately it wasn't your fault.'

Will lifted his dull eyes to the ceiling. 'Perhaps not, in the eyes of the law. But I haven't yet told you of the real coward in me.'

'Please go on.' Burrows squeezed his hand a little tighter, realising if he didn't get the full story while he was there, it might never be told at all. He fed him another sip of water, which only just made it down his throat.

'I never gave the tape to Mary. In my mind, she didn't deserve it. I hid it in my locker, together with the medical report, and it never saw the light of day until six weeks ago.'

'I guess it was difficult to listen to.'

'I am sure it was.'

'Will?'

'I never played it, Inspector.'

'You... never played it?'

'I told you I was a coward. I couldn't face listening to it, and it wasn't intended for me anyway. The poor private had been convicted, and for whatever reason had admitted to having an affair with Mary. I suspect his life was threatened. The whole thing had been quickly put to bed, the British army almost as content to let things be as the Ugandans. Everyone washed their hands of it.'

'Except you.'

'Oh, I washed my hands of it too. I could have told what I knew, handed over the tape and the medical report... but I didn't.'

'Why not?'

The tears rolled down his cheeks again. His face looked grey, lifeless. And yet somehow there was a sparkle of relief in his eyes. Burrows wiped away the tears for him. 'Take your time, Will.'

'I fear I do not have time, Inspector. You must understand how different things were back then, especially in the British army. Some saw Richard as living in a bygone era... pistols at dawn, and all that. But if they'd found out he'd taken his own life over a woman, that would have been seen as an act of cowardice. Most in the army would have shaken their heads and said he should have fought for his marriage. His reputation as a fine, upstanding man would have been sullied. I could not be responsible for allowing that to happen.'

'I can see that. But you still allowed an innocent man to be convicted. Well ok, he wasn't innocent, regardless of the circumstances. But he would have been charged with attempted murder, not actual murder. And even that might not have stuck, seeing as the man was already dead when he tried to murder him.'

'Why do you think I sent the tape and the medical report to his son, Inspector?'

It was clear why. But it had still taken William over fifty years to take that step. Burrows narrowed his eyes, but found it hard to be angry with the dying man. 'Why after so many years, Will?'

He found a little strength for a hoarse chuckle. 'Because I am a coward, Inspector. It was easier to let sleeping dogs lie. But it has lain heavy on me for all these years. Now my life is ending, I needed to absolve myself of the burden of a secret only I knew. It is selfish I realise, but nevertheless I wish to go to my maker knowing that at least I have put things right in the end.'

Burrows nodded his head. 'I can see your thinking. I just wish you hadn't left it so long.'

'You are not the only one..Believe me, if I could have lived my life again, I would have done things differently. Hindsight is a terrible burden sometimes, Inspector.'

'Why send it to Joseph's son? Why not the British army, or the Ugandan authorities?'

'Because both would just see it as raking up old wounds. Nothing would be done. I tried to find out if Joseph's wife was still alive, and her address. I could find neither. But Michael has a position at the Ministry of Internal Affairs, so it was easy enough to ask my sister to post it there.'

Once again Burrows was tempted to tell him Michael was dead, but the man was struggling to breathe again. He lifted the oxygen mask to his face once more, but this time it didn't seem to be making much difference. Will's eyes locked into his, a pleading kind of look that stabbed him through the heart.

'Will, I promise you we are doing all we can to put this right. But please, the name of the sergeant who was having the affair would help...'

Suddenly his head was shaking from side to side, as his lungs finally gave out. Then his eyes closed. He tried to speak, but the words came out as a strangled, incomprehensible gasp.

And then he was still.

Burrows pressed the emergency call button. In less than a minute two nurses ran into the room. He stepped away, allowed them space to do what they needed. Two frantic minutes went by, and then they stood back. One of them glanced over to him, shook her head.

'He's gone.'

DCI Burrows drove away from the Shady Oaks Nursing Home, fighting off the tears. The interview had been way more harrowing than he'd anticipated, and watching someone's life slip away was always a hard thing to do, total stranger or not.

The story he'd been told was tragic, in so many ways, and somehow that made Will's death harder to bear. Burrows realised the man had likely understated how much of a burden he'd spent much of his life bearing. The only one who knew the truth, he'd lived with keeping it a reluctant secret for over fifty years.

The reasons for his silence were in some ways understandable, yet today would seem so much less important. He'd remained loyal to his friend's memory, but it had clearly come at a great cost. For whatever reason Burrows would never know, once he knew his life was drawing to a close, he'd decided it was finally time to reveal the truth.

A truth someone clearly didn't want revealed. Will had gambled on Joseph's son being the best bet to ensure the truth was told, warts and all. That gamble had started a chain of events that in one way had paid off, but in another had cost Michael his life.

Will had gone to his grave believing he'd finally done the right thing.

As he left the cottages of Halesworth behind, Burrows shook his head in frustration. What he'd been told was hot news indeed, and once he'd transferred what was on the recorder to a flash drive and sent it to Lowry, she would know for sure just how important the conversation was.

But one crucial fact was missing. William Rushmore had died moments before revealing the name of the Ugandan sergeant who was having the affair with the captain's wife.

There was no way he could help with that. It was something his favourite pain in the butt was going to have to unearth for herself.

Chapter 17

Daisy, Aidan and Sarah sat in virtual silence in the dining room, forcing down nicely-cooked meals they didn't feel one bit like eating.

They were the only ones there. Hurrying down to eat through necessity rather than any desire to enjoy a nice meal, they made the dining room just a few minutes before closing time.

Listening to a man die had rather stolen away their appetites.

Burrows had mailed the recording of his interview with William Rushmore to Aidan's laptop, and as they'd sat listening to the deathbed confession, they'd all felt yet more unexpected and unwanted emotions.

Sarah toyed with the food on her plate. She'd hardly managed a single mouthful. 'That poor man.'

Daisy nodded her head. 'Let's get it in perspective though... it was a tragic story, but the man held onto a secret for over fifty years that could have exonerated Joseph.'

'Doesn't make it any easier to hear though. I know he would have still been convicted of attempted murder, but even so...'

Aidan smiled ruefully. 'Can you be convicted of attempting to murder a man who was dead one second before you tried to kill him?'

Daisy forced a piece of chicken into her mouth. 'I guess there's an argument on both sides of that. In the UK he would never have been convicted of murder, but in Uganda I'm not so sure.'

Sarah wiped away a tear, gave up on eating and pushed her plate away. 'You're forgetting someone forced him to do it though.'

Aidan put a hand on her arm. 'Try and eat a little more, Sarah. We're not forgetting that, because it's the very reason we're investigating this now.'

'And it's not got any easier.' Daisy shook her head with frustration. 'Burrows was a few seconds away from finding out who was having the affair when Will popped his clogs.'

'*Daisy!*'

'Sorry Sarah. Trying and failing dismally to keep the emotion out of it. I know that's impossible.'

'Yes, it is. Regardless of the fact he kept things secret that he shouldn't, he died an unpleasant death after struggling with what he knew for over fifty years.'

Daisy lowered her head. All too aware she had also kept secrets from people in the past, the tragic sadness of Will's life suddenly hit her. Aidan noticed, of course.

'You okay, dear?'

She nodded unconvincingly. 'Stupid bugger. Stupid so-called codes of honour. They should be made illegal.'

Aidan leant over, wrapped an arm around her shoulders. 'It's alright, Flower. That recording got to us all. The only thing we can do now is find the missing tape, make it right.'

'Yes, but where the hell is it? If Joseph had it on him when he died at my feet, I'm sure he would have handed it to me, instead of a scribbled note.'

A pretty Ugandan waitress sidled up to the table, asked them if they would like anything else, which was clearly code for *please leave now, so we can all go home.* Aidan smiled to her, speaking for them all. 'No, nothing else, thank you. We'll be gone in ten minutes.'

97

Daisy watched her walk away, no doubt to pass on the good news to the rest of the dining room staff. 'And the police didn't say anything about a cassette tape.'

Aidan chuckled mirthlessly. 'If they'd listened to it, we could maybe understand why.'

Daisy shook her head. 'No... Michael didn't have the tape on him. He must have realised it was a red flag. He's hidden it somewhere, while he investigated further, to make sure of the facts.'

'I think he was on the way to BATUK in Nairobi, to see what he could find out from there,' said Sarah.

'It makes sense. That's exactly what Anton did.'

Aidan was fitting more pegs into holes. 'That was why he said "no police" to you. He must already have known he'd been poisoned, and why.'

Daisy's eyes glazed over, appearing to focus on the far wall as she tossed around the new facts in her mind. 'Whoever that sergeant in the Ugandan Rifles was, he's still alive, and he's not a sergeant anymore.'

'You think he's risen through the ranks?' said Sarah.

'Sure of it. And he knows full well that even in Uganda, if it was proved he ordered a private to murder a British captain under threat of his life, it wouldn't exactly be good for him.'

'Only someone at the top of the military tree would have the resources to make sure it would never get out. Or murder someone with snake poison.'

Daisy sank the last of her wine. 'And guys... it's us three and Anton who it all comes down to now. We're the ones responsible for bringing this thug to justice... for two murders.'

'We need to find that tape,' said Aidan. 'Captain Mackenzie might have mentioned the sergeant's name on it.'

'That's a fair assumption, Dip. Maybe we should start at Michael's home? We just need to find out where he lived.'

Aidan stood up. 'Daisy, bring Anton up to speed in the morning. I'll get on the laptop, see if I can get some kind of address for Michael. But first we should try and find sleep. It's been a harrowing day to say the least, so perhaps we should put a lid on it.'

They left the dining room, but didn't notice the waitress waving them goodbye, in a slightly sarcastic but very relieved way.

Chapter 18

Daisy crawled reluctantly out of bed the next morning. It had been a night of fitful sleep, and she almost felt worse than before she'd crashed into bed. She flicked the kettle, emptied some sachets of coffee into mugs, and prodded a still-asleep Aidan.

'Wake up, you lazy lump. Coffee's brewed.'

'Go away.'

'Not the right answer. I'm anticipating more of a *'Yes dear. I'll get straight onto finding Michael's address.'*

She heard a muffled groan. 'Yes dear. I'll get straight onto finding Michael's address.'

'That's my boy. Drink your coffee, it'll help.'

He forced himself into a sitting position. 'What's making you so bright-eyed and bushy... *oh...*'

'Oh?'

'You don't exactly look bright-eyed and bushy-tailed.'

'Don't worry about it, dear. I still look better than you do.'

'Thanks for the compliment.'

'You do realise it's gone nine?'

'We are on holiday, Flower.'

'Yeah, right.'

'Ok, just thought I'd try that for size. I guess if I find Michael's address, that's today's sightseeing trip?'

'You wanted to see real Ugandan life.'

'Can I take that comment back please?'

Daisy grinned, watched as he padded to the bathroom, then took a long gulp of her coffee, and picked up the phone. Anton answered after a few seconds.

'How did Burrows get on?'

'He recorded the interview, so I'll get Aidan to send it to you in a few minutes. Just be warned, it doesn't make for easy listening.'

'How so?'

'William Rushmore died while Burrows was with him. It's all on the tape.'

'Shit. Sorry gal, but it seems like everyone's dying in this tale.'

'Tell me about it. He did manage to tell a revealing story before he died though. Six weeks ago he sent an old tape cassette and army medical report to Michael Ssebina. He'd finally decided to reveal the secret only he knew... and it was almost certainly why Michael was killed.'

'Geez... someone wants it to stay hidden. Where is the tape now?'

'No idea. We think it might be concealed somewhere at his home. Aidan is going to try and find an address right after he's sent the mail to you.'

Ok. I'll see if I can find it too, from this end.'

'Thanks, Anton. Call me later, when you've listened to the recording.'

An hour later he was back on the phone, letting out whistley sighs. *'Geez, Petal. Looks like you opened a hell of a can of worms here.'*

'I think that's an understatement, Anton. But in order to slam it on someone's desk, we've got to find that tape.'

'For sure. I doubt he'd hidden it at work, so the most likely place is his home. And I've done the homework too, if you like...'

'Plot 5, Kigobe Road, Ntinda?'

'I still reckon I'll get the better of you one day.'

101

'Have to credit Aidan with that one. He's just spent an hour trawling through the internet to find it.'

'Let me know how you and your hairpin get on.'

'Damn it, Anton. You know me so well.'

Another hour later they were grabbing a quick bite in the Red Basket cafe, having missed breakfast at the hotel. Then they walked a little way towards Ternan road, and found a group of minibuses waiting for fares from the visiting business-conference delegates.

Sarah breathed a sigh of relief as they were waved into the rear seats. 'I was getting visions of boda-bodas again.'

Daisy grinned, a silent admission she too was hardly keen to repeat the experience. 'There are three of us this time, dear,' was all she actually said.

They left the centre of Kampala, the driver, who was slightly older than their previous one, heading north-east on the Jinja highway at a respectable speed. He was experienced enough to know most muzungus weren't as easy to fool as his younger compatriots seemed to think they were.

Ten minutes later they made a left turn into a slightly-narrower road, drove for just over a mile and then turned onto Kigobe road at Ministers Village. A half-mile further on, the driver turned into a short unmade road, and pulled up outside a tall cement-rendered wall.

'You want me to wait?' he asked.

'No need, thanks. But if you come back in a couple of hours or so we would appreciate it,' said Aidan.

He nodded, and drove away.

'It's a detached bungalow... inside a wall,' said Sarah.

'Standalone, dear,' Daisy corrected. 'That's what they call them here. But I'm a little surprised the gates are open.'

'Maybe you won't need your hairpin after all, dear,' Aidan grinned.

They walked through the tall black metal gates, into a front garden full of tropical trees and neatly-trimmed bushes. The brick-weave drive was lined with edge-pavers, painted alternate black and white, and it curved round to a small forecourt fronting the orange and white walls of the medium-sized bungalow.

'Someone's here,' said Sarah quietly.

Sitting in front of the garage door was a white Toyota saloon. Daisy narrowed her eyes. 'By all accounts he wasn't married. Maybe he had a girlfriend?'

'Only one way to find out. Let's go and introduce ourselves. Won't be so easy to search the place now though.'

They walked up the three steps onto the long porch which ran half the length of the house. Edged with elegant painted balustrades, a few white tubs holding flowering plants were dotted around the raised, tiled floor. Daisy pressed a finger to the doorbell.

No one came. They were just beginning to think whoever was there didn't want to answer the door, when a latch bolt was drawn back, and the varnished door opened just a little. An elderly Ugandan woman peered out at them. 'Yes? Can I help you?'

Daisy smiled warmly. 'Hello. I'm Daisy Morrow. This is my husband Aidan, and my dear friend Sarah. We weren't expecting anyone to be home. Are you... a relative, please?'

The woman looked them up and down, didn't answer for a moment. Then she seemed to relax a little, and introduced herself.

'I'm Florence Matovu, Michael's mother.'

Chapter 19

Still the door wasn't open more than a foot. It wasn't difficult to understand why. Three muzungus on the doorstep of her dead son's house was a sight his mother wasn't expecting to see.

And now they'd come face to face with Joseph's wife, there weren't a lot of options to achieve what they'd come to do. Other than to tell the truth.

'I realise we're imposing, Mrs. Matovu, but we've come all the way from England to investigate something, which has progressed to involve Michael.'

'You know he is dead?'

'Yes. That is why we are here now.'

Still she didn't move. 'You police?'

'I...' Sarah started to say, until Aidan kicked her foot. Daisy smiled warmly again. 'We're not police, but we are... special investigators. May we come in, please? We did visit Joseph yesterday.'

That seemed to do the trick. Florence opened the door wider, stood aside. 'Please come in. But I am not sure what help I can be, or why you are investigating at all.'

They stepped into the white-tiled hallway. A small low unit sat next to the door, but other than that there wasn't much other furniture. Florence led them into a large sitting room, also with a tiled floor. A pair of sofas stood facing each other on a brightly-coloured rug, and a flat-screen TV sat on one wall, above a white-painted shelf.

Through a shaped arch that looked Indian-style, a mahogany dining table with six ornate chairs arranged around it stood in a smaller space. Its far wall was made up of sliding glass doors that opened onto a paved terrace, and a manicured lawn beyond that. A tall metal structure had been built in one corner of the garden, supporting a black plastic water tank sitting high off the ground.

Florence indicated for them to sit on one of the brown leather sofas. 'I am puzzled, Daisy. Why would you come all the way from England to investigate my son, when he simply died of a heart attack?'

Daisy's own heart missed a beat. Just like Joseph, his wife had not been told the truth. She glanced to Aidan, who nodded silently. Like Daisy, he knew there was no alternative now but to tell the truth.

Daisy sucked in a deep intake of humid air. The truth had been difficult enough for them to hear. It was going to be ten times harder for Florence to hear.

She caught the woman's curious stare. Perhaps a little older than herself, her face was creased with lines that gave away the burden she'd had to bear through her life. Still an attractive woman, the black eyes boring into her held an intelligence she didn't expect to see. Smartly dressed in a European style long red skirt and white blouse top, she had clearly made the best of a life without a husband to care for her. She spoke in perfect English, with only a hint of Ugandan accent.

It was obvious she was far too savvy to be fobbed off by half-truths.

'Mrs. Matovu...'

'Please, call me Florence.'

'Florence, the truth is we came to Uganda on another matter, but then we... got involved in your son's death. It seems it was not as straightforward as those close to him were led to believe.'

'I don't understand.'

'Perhaps we should start at the very beginning? Please tell us what you know about that night in nineteen-sixty-four.'

Florence's eyes opened wide. 'What has this got to do with my husband's crime?'

'Rather a lot, we believe, Please, first of all tell us what you know of back then.'

Her head lowered. 'It was the worst day of my life. Up to then, anyway. Joseph and I had been planning to marry, but then he lost his job so joined the Rifles. He was only seventeen, I was fifteen...'

She dabbed a handkerchief to her eyes. Daisy's heart thumped desolately for the poor woman. Even after all the years that had passed, it was still hard being forced to recall the horror. 'I'm sorry, Florence. It is important, otherwise we wouldn't put you through this.'

She smiled. 'It is okay. Just a little hard though, when I have tried to put that time out of my mind. Joseph had only been in the army three weeks. He did not come home that night, so I went to the barracks. We did not live far away at that time. I was told he had murdered a British army captain.'

'But you didn't believe it.'

'No. But then they allowed me to visit him in prison. He told me he had done it. I begged him to tell me why, and he said he had lost his head over a white woman.'

Aidan shook his head. 'You didn't believe that either.'

'Of course not. Joseph was faithful, loyal. Whatever his reasons, it was not because of another woman.'

'You seem very sure about that.'

'Daisy, I was young, naive and in love, but we had been strong friends for years. I always knew when he wasn't telling the truth, which was rarely. But this time he kept to his story, for all these years.'

'Tell me what happened next.'

'Joseph was convicted, sentenced to death. If it hadn't been for one of his sergeants pleading for him, he would have been executed. That sergeant saved his life, and then fought for us to be allowed to marry in prison. I was carrying our son, Michael.'

'That sergeant must have been a good man.'

'Yes. He is a general now. From time to time he would come to see me, and even give me money on occasions. I needed it, because life for me had turned very bad.'

Sarah seemed to be living Florence's sadness with her. 'Didn't your family help you?'

She laughed, a little sarcastically. 'You do not know Uganda, especially all those years ago. When Joseph was convicted and it all became public, my mother disowned me. I was carrying the child of an unfaithful murderer, and she was spat at in the street. Someone tried to burn down our house. A few people saw Joseph as a hero for killing a British officer, but most saw him as an infidel. That is why I reverted to my maiden name, to start again and avoid the hatred.'

'Oh my god... I can't believe that. What did you do then?'

'In a way, I was lucky. A good friend took me in. She was poor like us, but she also never believed Joseph was capable of being unfaithful. I had Michael at her home, and when he was old enough I was lucky again. I had spent the first years of his life educating myself, and applied for a job at the British embassy in Kampala. It was little more than making tea, but through the years I climbed the ladder, and ended up as the secretary to the PA of the ambassador himself.'

107

Sarah wiped away a tear. 'Go you, Florence,' she said quietly.

Daisy needed to know something for sure. 'So Joseph never told you the real reason he did what he did?'

She shook her head sadly. 'Never. I asked him a million times, but he stuck to his word. I still believe he was protecting someone.'

Daisy sucked in another deep breath. 'Florence, from what we have discovered, it appears he *was* protecting someone. Someone who was more important to him than anyone else. You.'

Chapter 20

Florence got to her feet, tried to smile. 'Please accept my apologies, I have not offered you any hospitality. Would you like some tea? I am sure Michael has some here.'

'Yes, please,' said Aidan. 'Florence, does what Daisy said not surprise you?'

She glanced back as she headed quickly into the kitchen. 'Yes, but it is one of the many scenarios I have considered for years. Please give me a moment.'

Sarah walked to the window, stood gazing out over the greenery of the front garden. 'It seems every interview we make is harder to endure. How much more horrific stuff is there going to be before this is over?'

'Perhaps a little more, Sarah dear. I'll try not to make it any harder for you than it has to be.'

She spun round, shook a desolate head. 'I'm not thinking about myself, Daisy. My heartstrings are being plucked for these poor people, not me.'

'I know exactly what you mean, dear. Anton's can of worms seems to consist of worms with fangs.'

Florence reappeared, carrying a tray of cups. Daisy sipped her milky tea. 'I have to tell you some things that will not be easy to hear, Florence.'

'I have already been through so much. Whatever you have to tell me, I doubt it will be a surprise.'

Daisy was about to say something along the lines of not betting on that, but she bit her lip. 'Before I do, I need your permission for my friends to look through Michael's personal belongings. We believe there is something hidden here that will help reveal the truth.'

Florence smiled. 'I came here to sort his belongings, a few minutes before you arrived. I have decided to rent out his house, so I came today to sort through his personal items. I have only just started, so nothing has really been moved yet. Please do what you wish, if it will help with the truth.'

'Thank you, Florence. I realise you have only just started sorting, but have you come across an old cassette tape, by any chance?'

She shook her head. 'No, but as I said, I only had time to pull a few things from the kitchen cupboards before you arrived.'

Daisy nodded to Aidan and Sarah, who left to search the house. Daisy turned back to Florence. 'Now I will tell you everything we know, but I must warn you some of it may be a little... upsetting.'

'Please, tell me what you have discovered.'

Daisy knew she had to start at the beginning of their trip to Uganda, which in one way was the worst place to start from Florence's point of view. She told her Michael had stumbled into the airport and died at her feet. Then she said the words she really didn't want to say.

'The next day we were told your son had been poisoned. He didn't have a heart attack, Florence.'

She dabbed her eyes again. 'Here the authorities often do not tell the truth. But why would they say he had died of a heart attack if he didn't?'

'Because of the tape we are searching for. Someone high up knew he was in possession of it, and that it would reveal a secret they didn't want revealing. Telling you the truth of why he died would have raised suspicions, and from what I see in you, you wouldn't have left them unanswered.'

110

She wrapped shaking hands around her cup. 'I see what you meant by things that would be hard to hear. But I still don't see what Michael had to do with it. He wasn't even born when... when it happened.'

Daisy brought her up to speed with the events as she knew them, including the harsh fact the tape had been sent to her son because the only man who knew the truth couldn't find her address.

She shook her head, her anger building. 'So you are telling me my son died because he was an innocent pawn on the board?'

Daisy lowered her head. Florence had hit a tragic nail on the head, and there was no alternative but to tell her she was right. 'I'm so sorry, but yes, he was dragged into it as an innocent bystander. We believe he was on his way to the BATUK HQ in Nairobi, most likely to see if he could find any more evidence to corroborate the tape.'

'And you are saying Joseph was ordered to kill the captain by the person who was really having the affair with his wife?'

'It looks that way. I would assume he was threatened with his life... and yours.'

Florence narrowed her eyes. 'But you do not know who it was?'

'Not yet. But I promise you we'll find out. One reason why we have to find the tape. The captain may have given his name on it.'

'You must tell me when you know. I will kill whoever it is myself.'

'And ruin the rest of your life? Florence, I know how you feel, but please let us deal with it. The police in England are already involved, and... well, I have ways of bringing those to justice who deserve punishment.'

'In Uganda? Whoever it is must live in high places. He will consider himself untouchable.'

'Yeah well, he hasn't met me yet.'

Aidan and Sarah reappeared. In Aidan's hand was a large manila envelope. 'Found it taped under the kneehole in the desk in his office.'

'Can't find anything to play it on though,' said Sarah regretfully.

'Ok. We'll get back to the hotel, see if we can find an old player somewhere.' Daisy turned to Florence, took her hand. 'Will you be ok?'

'I am due a visit with Joseph on Thursday. I will give him the news of Michael, but I would like to be able to give him better news too. If you can somehow make the authorities aware of the truth, will it help Joseph's sentence?'

Aidan lifted his hands from his sides. 'I can't lie, in England his sentence would be reduced to attempted murder. He would already have served more time than he should. But in Uganda...'

'I understand. Please, take my phone number. I wish to be kept informed of your progress, please?'

She was begging, and Daisy knew she couldn't deny her request. Her innocent son had been murdered, but his murder could well help exonerate her husband, and convict the real criminal of two crimes. Daisy was well aware she herself would be chomping at the bit to make sure revenge was exacted. 'Sure, Florence. But please, don't do anything rash... not yet anyway.'

Florence walked with her guests to the front door. Daisy gave her a hug. 'I'll call you tomorrow, when we've hopefully had chance to listen to the tape. Keep smiling, yes?'

112

She nodded, her eyes misted by the truth about her son's death, but somehow sparkling with life because after all the years that had passed, someone was on her side who was prepared to stand up for what she'd always believed.

Daisy turned away to head down the steps, but then had a thought. 'Florence, that sergeant who befriended Joseph when he was convicted. What was his name?'

She smiled, recalling his compassion. 'His name was Oyite Emmanuel.'

They walked the short distance to Kigobe road, stood in the shade of a big leafy tree waiting for the taxi to return.

'What are you smiling about?' Aidan asked Daisy.

'I did tell you.'

'Tell us what?' asked Sarah.

'Who was the villain in all this.'

'Dear, just because you picked a random name out of a hat...'

'It was a random name out of my *gut*, Dip.'

He sighed. 'I suppose it is a bit of a coincidence. One of the big-wigs on Anton's list was a sergeant back then. But why would he show compassion to a private convicted of murder, and his wife?'

'Guilt, dear. Guilt. I doubt he feels the same now, after all these years. But right after it happened, he was still a young man who ordered someone to commit a crime of his passion. And there might have been another reason.'

Sarah, her police training putting her on the same wavelength, nodded her head. 'If it *was* him, he wouldn't be the first criminal to keep his victim's relatives sweet, to make sure they didn't suspect anything.'

'Exactly.'

113

'Let's just see if there's a name on this tape before we descend into the realms of wild speculation,' said Aidan cautiously.

Chapter 21

As soon as they reached the hotel, Aidan walked up to the reception desk and waved the tape at the young receptionist.

'Do you have anything that will play this, please?'

She narrowed her eyes. 'What is it, sir?'

Slightly taken aback, he stuttered, 'Its... it's a cassette tape. Like they used to record music onto, years ago.'

'Um... sorry, sir. This is a modern hotel.'

'Bugger.' He glanced round to Daisy, who didn't look too surprised. But then, a guy in chef's whites who had just walked through the rear door spoke up. 'Wow... an old cassette. Not many of those around these days.'

'Tell me about it. Trying to find something to play it on.'

The guy grinned. 'This might be a modern hotel, but the kitchen is a good old-fashioned sweat box. We still play music on an old cassette player, when the big boss ain't around.'

'I don't suppose I could...'

'I'll get it for you. Just drop it back to reception as soon as you can. Evening meal prep starts soon.'

He was gone. Three minutes later he was back, handing the small black machine to Aidan. 'Just remember I did you a favour, ok?'

Aidan slipped him a couple of notes from his shorts pocket. 'Thank you, so much. You're a life-saver. Well, you might be.'

In the room, Daisy asked Aidan to rig up the laptop as well as the old cassette player. 'Can we somehow record it onto the laptop? Then we'll have it logged, and we can send it to Anton.'

'We can, but it'll have to be through the lappy microphone. You'll have to keep quiet while we play it, or it'll pick up anything you say as well.'

As it turned out, keeping quiet wasn't a problem. As soon as the tape was loaded into the machine and Aidan pressed play, the sheer desolation in the captain's voice meant no one felt like uttering a word.

The recording was scratchy, and a little muffled by the passage of time. But the words, spoken in the clipped English manner of the era, were plenty clear enough to pluck heartstrings yet again...

'Hello, my dear. Although calling you that is perhaps a misnomer. I suspect these words will mean little to you, but regardless, it is the last time you will hear my voice.

'Your revelations last night were, as I am sure you are aware, devastating for me to hear. Too devastating to live with. To hear you admit to having an affair was the noose around my neck. To be told it was with a lowly Ugandan sergeant was the trap-door that opened beneath my feet.

'Mary, you must have known that for a principled man like myself, who insists on absolute loyalty, your confession was my gallows. I do not possess a noose or the means to hang myself, but here at Jinja barracks, the location of your infidelity, the tools to end my life are readily available.

'I will never know if you will mourn my loss, or if it will come as some relief for you and the man who has stolen your heart, but I want you to know this. I have always been faithful to you, and have not so much looked at another woman since we have been married. I always loved you, and despite what you have done, I always will.

116

'I expected you to be faithful, and never dreamt you would be anything but. I realise now that was a vain, naive hope. My dear friend William is about to bring me a hand grenade, and once I give him this tape and order him to leave, I will hold it to my chest and detonate it.

'I ask you to forgive me my weakness of spirit, but a life without you is a life I do not wish to live. Yet I go to my grave with a clear conscience, in the knowledge I have always held our vows in the true spirit they were intended. Goodbye, Mary.'

No one spoke. Aidan switched off the tape, and then closed the recording on the laptop. It was a full two minutes until Sarah broke the silence.

'I don't know how much more of this I can take,' she whispered.

Daisy nodded silently, unable to find any comforting words. Then she spoke to Aidan. 'Dear, please will you mail the recording to Anton. He needs to hear it.'

He nodded silently. Daisy walked slowly onto the balcony, leant her elbows on the rail and gazed out across the city to the smart houses lining the hill that was Kololo. Then she felt Aidan's arms around her waist.

'So do you still think I'm putting two and two together and making five, dear?' she whispered.

It was a moment before he answered. 'No. Your maths are impeccable as always, Flower. They definitely make four.'

She turned to him, held him tight. 'Thank you. That evil man caused the death of three people, and ruined the lives of two others. And now he lives in untouchable luxury, less than a mile from here. It just isn't fair, Dip.'

117

'The captain didn't mention a name on the tape though, unfortunately.'

'No, but general Oyite doesn't know that.'

He pressed her head into his shoulder, heard her let out a little sob, kissed her hair softly. 'It seems he got a taste for white women early in his life. We still don't know for sure, but if it was him who bought Celia, it would be logical.'

Daisy eased herself away, glared out again at Kololo hill. 'I know for sure it's him. Take me and feed me, dear. For what I'm going to do tonight, I need all the strength I can find.'

Chapter 22

'I'm really not happy about this.'

'Neither am I,' Sarah pouted.

'So what else do you suggest?' said Daisy sharply.

The three of them were taking an early dinner in the dining room, much to the relief of the waiting staff, who were glad it wouldn't be another late one. The sun was just disappearing over the horizon as Daisy devoured a three-course meal, an all-encompassing anger and determination to see her plan through prompting the hunger for food, as well as for justice.

The plan, such as it was, didn't exactly give Aidan and Sarah the same appetite. Both of them knew Daisy was running on emotion-fuelled adrenaline, which wasn't the ideal scenario for someone who got a little crazy at times anyway.

Or someone who would do whatever it took to get her daughter back, regardless of the consequences for herself.

'There has to be a... less risky way, dear.'

'So lay it on the table then.'

'I... I can't, not right now. I don't know what it is.'

Daisy leant forward, a steely glint in her eye. 'This is about our daughter, Dip. Well it was, originally. Now it's also about god knows how many other people, and bringing an evil man to justice. You think I won't risk everything for Celia, and Joseph and Florence too?'

He reached out, wrapped a hand around hers. 'I know you'll risk everything, dear. But we have to make it right, and somehow come out of it in one piece.'

Daisy shook her head. 'You've heard almost everyone we've spoken to. Emmanuel Oyite is untouchable, through

119

official channels at least. I have to force his hand, make him do something that can't be argued with.'

'And you think confronting him in his home this evening is going to achieve that?'

'Yes, I do. Don't you?'

'Sadly, yes. That's what's petrifying me.'

'If I convince him I have irrefutable proof he ordered Joseph to kill the captain and then murdered Michael, he'll have to make a move to shut me up. And while I'm there, I might... I might see Celia.'

Daisy's eyes dropped to her lap, and a trembling hand wiped away a tear. Aidan put his arm around her shoulder. 'I know you'll do everything to put this right, Flower. So despite my misgivings, I'm right there beside you.'

'And me,' said Sarah.

Daisy looked up quickly, shook her head, 'Dip, I can't ask you to risk your life. And you Sarah, you're definitely not coming.'

'*What?*'

'I mean it. This started out as a family matter, and I know it got complicated as soon as we landed here, but it doesn't alter the fact the main reason I'm doing what I am tonight is because of Celia. You have become like family to us, Sarah... but you're not *actual* family. Please tell me you understand?'

'Maybe.'

'And there's another reason. I doubt the general will risk doing anything to me in his own home, but if... if anything does happen, you're the police officer amongst us. It might then be up to you, and only you.'

'Oh Daisy... I can't bear to think...'

'As I said, I can't see it coming to that. But we have to cross all the T's, don't we?'

'I suppose so.'

Aidan locked his gaze into Daisy's misty eyes. 'And you needn't think for one second I'm letting you go alone, dear. As you said, Celia is our daughter. We'll both go into the lion's den... again.'

Daisy nodded slowly, and a little gratefully. 'Thank you, dear. Somehow I didn't think I'd be allowed to go alone.'

Back in the room, Daisy took a little while getting herself ready, and avoiding Sarah's glares. She and Aidan spent a few minutes talking through how they'd approach confronting the general, but didn't let Sarah hear any of the conversation, much to her annoyance.

'Am I not part of this anymore?'

Daisy pulled her into a hug. 'Of course you are, Sarah. But we need you kept out of tonight, so you can...'

'Make it official if you don't come back?'

Daisy let out a laugh she certainly wasn't feeling. 'Now you're being over-dramatic. Emmanuel Oyite won't do anything in his own home. But I want you to stay alert when we're gone. Don't open your door to anyone except us, ok?'

'You really are scaring me, Daisy.'

'Dear, it's just about taking every precaution. Just in case.'

The time clicked to just past eight. Aidan had called the reception desk, asked them to request a taxi. It was just a short distance to the general's luxury residence at Kololo, but they sure didn't feel like walking.

The phone buzzed, the receptionist informing them the taxi was waiting. Daisy asked Sarah for her phone. She handed it over.

'I'm giving you Anton's number, so you can contact him if... if you need to.'

121

'Daisy, please don't do this...'

Daisy turned away, picked up the cassette tape and slipped it into her coat pocket. She looked pointedly at Aidan. 'Give Sarah the laptop. Apart from this tape, the only record of Mackenzie's last words is on there.' She looked at Sarah. 'Go to your room now, dear. And hide the laptop, under the mattress or something. Just in case.'

She virtually bundled a still-protesting Sarah back to her room, and then handed her the key to their room. 'Take this, in case we... lose it or something. As soon as we're back, we'll come to you. Just watch a little TV, and try to relax. We'll be back in a couple of hours.'

'You'd better be.'

Daisy slipped her arm into Aidan's, and together they headed across the carpeted open walkway to the elevator. Daisy didn't look back, knowing Sarah was watching them go.

Glancing back at her petrified face would not have helped the determination to do whatever it took to make everything right.

Chapter 23

The taxi driver pulled up outside a house on leafy Kololo Hill Drive. It looked more like a fortress. A short driveway leading from the road had a sentry box standing next to it. Just beyond that, big grey fortified gates were set into a twelve-foot concrete wall, blocking out any view of what was beyond it.

Aidan whispered in an awestruck kind of way. 'Crikey… what's he so afraid of?'

'Us, hopefully.'

'Or anti-military coups. We might get in, but getting out again could be a problem.'

'He wouldn't dare.'

'I'll take your word for that.'

Aidan paid the taxi driver, who then drove away. Suddenly they felt very alone. The elegant tree-lined road had no streetlamps, but each of the up-market houses had their own lamps burning away in their gateways. And each had their own high walls, making it difficult to see anything that resembled civilization.

It was nine in the evening, and totally dark. Not a soul was around, and the lamps that did shine from entranceways did little other than emphasise the fact there were menacing dark shadows everywhere. Beyond the houses on the opposite side of the road, the lights of Kampala city stretched out below them into the distance. They were less than a mile away, but somehow it seemed like a million.

Daisy felt herself shiver, tried to shake away the feeling of apprehension. It wouldn't do to let Aidan see she was terrified. And even less of a good idea to let the general see it. She slipped an arm into his, and headed quickly to the sentry box.

A young soldier in Ugandan army uniform sat at a tiny desk, watching something on an equally-tiny screen. He looked up, a little shocked to see anyone standing next to the open window, staring at him.

Especially two elderly muzungus.

He pulled himself together, grabbed his automatic rifle and tried to look official. 'Yes? Can I help you?'

'We'd like to see General Oyite Emmanuel, please,' said Aidan firmly.

Um... the general doesn't take visitors at home, at this hour.'

'At this hour? It's nine o'clock.'

'I'm sorry. I can't allow you access.'

Daisy gave him the glare. 'Do you have communications equipment in this box?'

He glanced inadvertently to the telephone on the desk, which Daisy had already spotted. 'Um... yes, but the general will not be pleased to be disturbed.'

'Tough. Tell him we're here to see him, please.'

He reached slowly for the handset. 'Are you... friends of his?'

'No. We're his worst nightmare.'

Aidan put a hand on Daisy's arm, gave the guard a fake smile. 'Tell him Daisy and Aidan Henderson are here to see him, on a matter of extreme urgency. I think you'll find he'll wish to speak with us.'

Daisy threw him a narrow-eyed stare. 'He doesn't even know who we are, Dip.'

'Doesn't he? I suspect you're about to discover the police and the military are joined at the hip here, dear.'

The guard was speaking in Luganda to someone. Then he went silent, like he was waiting for instructions. One minute went by, which Daisy spent jigging up and down, wishing she'd brought her gun. Then finally he spoke.

'The general will see you now. Please proceed to the main entrance of the house, where someone will meet you.'

He pressed a button on a keypad on his arm, and the heavy gates clicked and began to open.

'About time,' Daisy couldn't help growling as she and Aidan made their way into the compound, her less adrenaline-fuelled husband leading her away before she said something she really shouldn't.

They could hardly see the white-painted two-storey house, the circular drive curling through a hundred palm trees masking a clear view of the elegant pillared entrance, which looked like it would be more at home at the White House. The entire frontage of the house was lit by floodlights, and tall lamps spaced around the paved forecourt made sure no one got close without being picked up by the myriad of CCTV cameras dotted around the compound.

Daisy shook her head to Aidan as they walked up the long drive. 'How the evil half live, hey dear?'

He nodded his agreement but didn't say anything, just pointed to a single-storey building sitting to one side of the main house. Lights shone from its windows, and it didn't need more than one guess to work out it was the living quarters of a small army of security guards.

They reached the opulent double mahogany doors, and Aidan was just about to ring the doorbell when one of the doors swung open. Someone was standing there, who had clearly been instructed to watch them arrive.

She was pretty, blonde-haired, and white-skinned.
But she wasn't Celia.

'Please, do come in.'

They walked into a big, grand entrance hall. A pristine white tiled floor seemed to have a hundred shiny wood doors leading off it. A wide, carpeted staircase with gold statues for newel posts stretched up to a galleried landing, giving access to the upstairs rooms. A huge gold chandelier hung from the high ceiling, with sixty bright light-bulbs reflecting off jewelled glass spheres, illuminating the space in a dazzling glow of ever-changing light.

The woman led them to one of the doors. 'I am Alice, the general's chief housekeeper. He will see you in the study. Please go in.'

She reached out an elegant hand to the gold-plated circular knob, and eased the door open. Daisy and Aidan stepped into the room, doing their best not to show their distaste. The so-called study was almost as big as their cottage, furnished entirely with expensive solid wood furniture, apart from two Queen-Anne chintz sofas sitting on a plain blue rug.

The flock-papered walls were adorned with framed portraits of military leaders through the ages. Daisy noticed one of Museveni and the general, pictured together. A huge, indoor palm sat in a low, metre-wide tub in one corner, and tall units with open-shelved tops filled with books ran around two walls. Close to the far wall, a long, elaborately-shaped solid wood desk had a huge Ugandan flag standing behind it, and a stocky Ugandan man pouring himself a drink in front of it.

He turned as his guests walked into the room, and gave them a big, false smile. He was wearing a black silk gown with gold lapels, and simple open sandals on his feet. And somehow, the lack of a military uniform or an array of shiny medals made the false smile seem even more menacing.

He was clearly getting on in years, his craggy, lined face and cropped grey hair emphasising his advancing age, and the fact he'd seen more than his fair share of military conflict. The cold, dark eyes accentuated something else, which the false smile was trying but failing to disguise.

'Mr. and Mrs. Henderson,' he said in a deep, husky voice. 'It is a pleasure to meet you. What can I do to help?'

Before Aidan could stop her, Daisy threw him an even-more false smile, and blurted it out in one short sentence.

'We'd like our daughter back, please.'

Chapter 24

The general froze, just for a moment, but then the fake smile was back.

'Now what on Earth leads you to believe a man in my position needs to *kidnap* a woman, Mrs. Henderson?'

Aidan looked at Daisy in horror, but she'd started so she was sure as hell going to finish. 'Oh General Oyite, I've no doubt you have no need to steal a *local* girl… but that's not what floats your boat, is it?'

He shook his head, almost imperceptibly, and then lifted his crystal glass. 'Forgive me, I have not offered you a drink. It is the finest Courvoisier, can I persuade you?'

'No thanks. Just answer the question.'

'I am not familiar with the phrase *floating my boat*, I am afraid.'

'Of course you are. You've had plenty of years to get to know English girls, so don't tell me you have no idea what I'm talking about.'

His eyes narrowed menacingly. 'If you are referring to my preference for white women, that is no business of yours, dear lady.'

Aidan tried to stop her, but Daisy was already striding towards him, flames of desperate anger in her eyes. 'Oh, it is my business when you *buy* my daughter, you sick piece of shit.'

He stepped back a little, shocked by the fury spat out at him. He looked across to Aidan. 'Please, Mr. Henderson, control your wife. I fear she is a little mentally disturbed.'

Aidan wrapped firm hands around Daisy's arms, and pulled her back a little, still glaring evils into the general's eyes. *'Cool it, dear. This isn't helping,'* he said quietly, and then spoke a little louder to the general. 'My wife is disturbed, but not mentally. In truth we are both disturbed, by what has recently come to light.'

That got the general's attention. His narrowed eyes opened wider. The words were spoken cautiously. 'What do you mean by that?'

'Just that we have irrefutable proof it was *you* who had the affair with the British captain's wife at Jinja barracks in nineteen-sixty-four, and it was you who ordered Joseph Ssebina to do your dirty work for you. And we also know it was you who instigated the poisoning of his son.'

The general's eyes narrowed to suspicious slits again. He didn't seem too surprised at being reminded of a crime committed many years ago, but took his time putting his glass down on the desk, and only then turned to face Aidan and answer his allegations. 'Whatever proof you think you have, Mr. Henderson, I can assure you it is falsified information.'

'Oh, I see. And how sure are you of your words, General?'

He took a moment to answer, like he was searching for the right thing to say. 'Perhaps you should show me what alleged proof you have, and then we will all know it is fantasy.'

He'd not even glanced to Daisy since Aidan had pulled her away. That didn't sit too easily in Daisy's world, being dismissed as irrelevant by a man who likely treated all women the same, unless they were young and pretty. She reached into her coat pocket, pulled out the tape, and waved it in front of his face, so he couldn't ignore her anymore.

'See this, General? It's what got Michael Ssebina killed, wasn't it? But I've got big news for you.'

129

He watched the tape waving in front of his eyes, like it was trying to hypnotise him. 'What are you saying, Mrs. Henderson?'

'Wouldn't you like to know.'

'Actually, yes I would like to know what fantasy you believe is reality. You think I am scared of an old white woman, Mrs, Henderson?'

Daisy put her face right next to his. 'I haven't said *boo* yet.'

She moved back a little, still glaring the glare into him like she hated every fibre of his body. 'But you might like to know, that murder you got Joseph to commit... it wasn't necessary, and it *wasn't* murder.'

He turned away, picked up the glass and sank the Courvoisier in one gulp. Then he turned back, and Daisy could see the beads of sweat on his brow. 'How... you can't possibly... I heard the explosion. They arrested Joseph, he admitted...'

'Admitted it was him having the affair, because you told him he was a dead man if he didn't?'

'I... you cannot prove this...'

'Ah, but I can, General.' Daisy waved the tape a little nearer to his face again. 'This proves it. It's a tape Richard Mackenzie made right before he died. You see, Mary confessed to her husband the previous night that she was having an affair with you. The captain couldn't handle her cheating, so he made this tape explaining it all, and saying goodbye to his wife.'

'Goodbye?' he whispered hoarsely.

'Did you not see Mary again after that night, General?'

'No... we had decided not to meet for a couple of days. But I was told the next day she left the barracks. I never saw her again...' He hitched his breath, suddenly realising what he was admitting. 'We... knew each other, that was all.'

He poured himself another brandy, sank it in a single swig. Daisy knew then she'd got him where she wanted him.

'So you don't know the captain killed himself?'

'*What?* No, that is not possible...'

Daisy threw him a mirthless grin, stuck the tape even closer to his dark eyes. 'You listen good, General. This tape tells it all, including the fact Richard Mackenzie held a grenade to his chest and detonated it, one second before Joseph's grenade went off. So you see, you murdering piece of crap, you didn't need to order a rookie private to do it.'

'*No...*' He froze for a second, the fact slamming home he'd not only lost the white girl he wanted for himself, but had also ordered a murder he didn't need to. One second later he unfroze himself, tried to grab the tape from Daisy's hand. '*Give me that...*'

She was too quick for his lunge, even though she had every intention of letting him have it when she was ready. Aidan stepped between them, protecting his wife.

'So let me get this clear, General. You are admitting to us you were the one having the affair with Mackenzie's wife, and the person who ordered Joseph Ssebina to kill him?'

The general turned back to his desk. Clearly shocked by the revelations he'd had no previous knowledge of, he nevertheless still believed no one actually knew the truth. No one who was still alive to tell the tale, apart from the three people in the room.

And it was still possible to make it so two of them never made it public knowledge.

He sat down in the elegant leather chair behind the desk, let out a little chuckle. 'You are indeed brave to come here this night, Mr. and Mrs. Henderson. But perhaps also a little foolish. I will tell you the truth, as you already seem to know it, for what good it will do you. My position in the military establishment of this country means I can make things... go away, if you understand me.'

'So now you make threats. Hardy surprising, for a man like you.'

He smiled like someone who thought he held all the cards. 'The truth is I did fall in love with Mary. I was young, a little naive, and willing to believe she would leave the captain for me. Somewhat foolishly, as it turns out. And I was desperate enough to... enlist the help of a private to murder the captain. Again rather foolishly, as it also turns out, as I am now informed the captain took his own life anyway.'

'So you really made a mess of things.'

'Perhaps. But in my defence, I felt guilty for what I'd done... or tried to do, as I have discovered tonight. I pleaded for Joseph's life, and arranged for him and his wife to marry in prison.'

'Yes, we know. We spoke to Florence yesterday. She was of the opinion you were benevolent.'

His eyes opened wide again. 'I see your investigation has been thorough.'

Aidan nodded. 'But there is one thing we don't know. You were clearly aware Michael had new evidence, but how?'

The general shook his head. 'Like you, he came to confront me, a week ago. The foolish man tried to intimidate me, tell me he had been informed of new evidence that would incriminate me. I did not believe him, but I could not be sure.'

'So you poisoned him... to *be* sure.'

'Please, Mrs. Henderson, give me that tape, and you will not be harmed. You must understand that in Uganda, those at the top of the military tree will always survive such past demeanours.'

Daisy walked up to the desk, placed the tape in front of the general. She noticed him reach under the kneehole, and knew exactly what he was doing.

At any moment they would not be the only people in the room.

The general smiled and picked up the tape, in a relieved kind of way. 'Thank you. And now I must retire to my bed. My men will escort you back to your hotel.'

'Yeah, I bet they will,' Daisy hissed to Aidan under her breath.

The shiny wooden door opened, and four guards clomped into the room. Each one sported a stony-faced expression, and a fearsome-looking automatic rifle. The general issued his instructions. 'Please drive my friends back to their hotel, and ensure they do not meet with any unfortunate accidents.'

It was clearly a code they understood meant something else entirely. Daisy glanced to Aidan, as he slipped an arm around her.

'Oh dear, dear,' she whispered dejectedly.

Chapter 25

Sarah sat on her bed, idly flicking the TV remote. For a whole five minutes.

Then sitting in one place got too much to take, so she stepped out onto her balcony, and spent another two minutes gazing out at Kololo Hill, wondering how her friends were getting on.

That was an understatement. The fear for Daisy and Aidan's safety thumped pulses of unease through her, and each one seemed to be filling her head with a more horrific scenario than the last. And gazing at the place where they were putting their lives in danger wasn't helping.

Daisy's actions before they'd left hadn't helped her state of mind either. Asking her to hide the laptop, giving her the key to their room... making sure she had Anton's phone number. It all seemed a bit... final.

Anton.

She walked slowly back into the room, picked up her phone. Her finger hesitated over the call button. Would he think she was just being a rookie cop, lacking faith that Daisy could handle herself? He would likely just say what Daisy had already said, tell her to watch a little TV and chill out.

She couldn't chill out. Watching TV like an obedient granddaughter wasn't an option for Officer Sarah Lowry.

She pressed call. After a few seconds Anton's voice answered, a little hesitantly. *'Yes?'*

'Anton, it's Sarah, Daisy and Aidan's friend. Sorry to disturb you.'

He didn't speak for a second. *'Hey, Sarah. Is everything okay?'*

'Not really. Well, it might not be. I don't know. That's why I called you.'

'What's wrong?'

She told him where Daisy and Aidan had gone, and what they were trying to achieve. And his reaction sent more thumps of dread through her heart.

'Geez, are they insane? Daisy said she would do whatever it took to get Celia back, but this?'

'Anton, I tried to persuade them not to do it, but you know what Daisy's like. And now you're terrifying me even more.'

'Hell, girl. Sorry, but… oh crap, I shouldn't tell you this, but I did a bit of research into the general, coz Daisy seemed so sure he was the one. Apparently he's a real tyrant, half of Uganda is shit scared of him. One of the real hard-liners… even Museveni himself has had to reprimand him a couple of times in the last year or two, for… overstepping the mark, shall we say.'

'You're not exactly filling me with joy here, Anton.'

'Ok look, I'll get myself over there, but there are no flights now 'til morning. Ain't nothing I can do right now kid, so's you're just gonna have to hope for the best. We can't intervene officially without concrete proof.'

'I can't just sit here and hope for the best, Anton. Have you got his address?'

'Yes, but…'

'Give it to me, please.'

'Sarah, what are you going to do..?'

'Give me the address, please,' she said sharply.

He gave it to her, reluctantly. *'You can't just go steaming in there alone, girl.'*

'I… I won't be alone. There's someone here who… who will help.'

135

'Who?'

She killed the call, raised her eyes to the ceiling in frustration. She hadn't exactly been honest with Anton. She didn't know if the someone would actually help, but in a strange country, with her friends in danger and Anton a long way away, it was all she had.

The last person she really wanted to see again.

She pulled out the little card from her bag, shook her head again at the wording on it. Then she dialled the number. A cheery voice answered.

'*Hey there, Will.i.is at your service. Taking you to places...*'

'Hello, Will. It's Sarah.'

'*S...Sarah? The police chick?*'

'Um, yes... if you like.'

'*Hey girl, you changed your mind? I's just finishing up with a client, then I'm all yours. We gonna have one hell of a night, bank on it.*'

'Will... we're going to have a hell of a night, but not in the way you think. I'm afraid I have to ask for your help. 'Um... official police business. I need your wheels, and I... I need you.'

'*Hey, ain't no need to be afraid, girl...*'

'Oh there is, trust me.'

'*You want me to be a deputy... of the British police?*'

'Well...' Sarah thought quickly. She had no official jurisdiction in Uganda, but Wilfred didn't know that. If he thought he was deputised, it might ensure his full cooperation.

'Yes... yes, I do, Will. But I have to warn you it might be... a bit scary.'

'*Hey girl, they don't call me The Rock for nothin' you know.*'

Sarah threw her eyes to the cracked ceiling again. The boy was all of nine stone. But, as she reminded herself, right then he was all she'd got. 'Can you get here now, Wilfred? Meet you outside in fifteen? We need to go somewhere in Kololo.'

'*On my way, boss. Geez, this is exciting!*'

'That's my line.'

Sarah slipped the key into Daisy's door, delved into the bottom of the wardrobe and pulled out the sports bag. She groaned to herself, asked her head what the hell she was doing. It wasn't difficult to answer her own silent question.

In the general's military world, an automatic rifle spoke volumes. If she was going to help her friends at all, being armed and dangerous might be the only way to get them out in one piece. She pulled out the gun, loaded a magazine into it, and then dropped it into the bottom of the bag and covered it with the towels.

She'd had basic weapon instruction in her police training, but it was basic, to say the least. She'd only fired a gun in anger once before, and that time hadn't ended so well. She'd managed to destroy a fishing cruiser by accident, together with the lives of two criminals. It hadn't sat easy with her, and was one of the reasons Daisy and Aidan had insisted to Burrows she took compassionate leave.

Which in turn was one of the reasons she was in Uganda at all.

She shook her head and left the room, doing her best to convince herself that in the world she was about to walk into, a lethal weapon was an absolute necessity.

She walked across the ground floor with the sports bad slung over her shoulder, feeling like a criminal, and praying no one had x-ray vision and could see what was inside the innocent-looking bag.

No one did of course; the ground floor was almost deserted. She quickened her step as she made the outside door, grateful to see the Nissan minibus waiting for her just outside. She almost fell into the passenger seat, and was met by Wilfred's grinning face.

'Hey, boss. We undercover cops or something now?'

'Um... yes, Will. We need to get to Kololo, quick.'

He floored the throttle, relishing his instant new role in life. 'Hey, do I get a badge, boss?'

'Just drive.'

Chapter 26

Wilfred's boyish enthusiasm died a little as they turned into Kololo Hill Drive, and Sarah told him where they were going.

'General Oyite's place? Hell boss, you sure know how to pick 'em.'

'You been here before?'

'You kidding me? Not a chance in hell, girl. But everyone in Kampala know he's one big fish you don't mess with.'

'Well, I'm about to mess with him. You're welcome to just drop me at the gate and leave. It might get a bit hairy, and I can't force you to stick around.'

'Seriously? I's got a duty to you, boss. Especially now I's an undercover cop.'

Sarah couldn't help letting out a smile. She had to admit to herself that for the first time she was really glad to be in Wilfred's company.

She pulled the rifle from the bag. Wilfred's eyes opened wide. '*Whoa, girl*. You is full of surprises. Where you get an RPKS-74 from?'

It was Sarah's turn for the wide eyes. 'You know what this is?'

'Hell, yeah. They's all over the place here. This is Africa, baby.'

'Don't call me baby.'

'Sorry, boss. You got one of them for me?'

'Absolutely not... but I'll tell you what, you can hold it when we get inside the compound. Just keep the safety on. No shooting, ok?'

'Aw, come on, ba... boss. That ain't no fun.'

'We're professionals, not here for fun. No shooting, ok?'

'Just one bullet?'

'Definitely not. That... thing is just here to make a point.'

'You the boss,' Wilfred said reluctantly.

The Nissan pulled up alongside the tiny guard hut. Sarah leant out of the window, flashed her badge. 'Officer Lowry, British police. Let us in, please.'

The young guard threw a disbelieving look at the third white-skinned visitor in less than an hour. 'Um... I don't think the general wants any more visitors tonight, miss.'

'I'm sure he doesn't. But he's got them, regardless. Open the gates, please.'

'Have you... um, got an appointment?'

Sarah was just about to bring the rifle into play and point out she didn't need an appointment, but then Wilfred leant over, a big grin on his face. 'Hey, Buk... is that you?'

The young guard stepped out of his hut, leant his face close to the open window. 'Wilfred? That you?'

'Hey man, how's you doing?'

'You know him?' said Sarah incredulously.

'Sure. We was at school together in Namugongo, la... a while back.'

'What you doing, Will? You working for the police now?'

'Sure I am. We's on an undercover operation.'

'Man, I thought you was just driving a taxi. How'd you get that gig then?'

'Hey, you know me, man. Always take an opportunity, if it's there on the table.'

'Respect to you, bro. How long you been doing this then?'

'Will... the operation, remember?' said Sarah.

'Hey boss, just catching up with my man here. How long you been in the military then, Buk?'

'Wilfred... time is of the essence, please?'

140

'Oh yeah, sure boss. Hey Buk, you gotta let us in, man. Matter of life and death, and all that?'

'Geez Will, I don't know. I need this gig.'

'If you don't let us in, you might not have a gig anyway,' said Sarah sharply.

Wilfred grinned to his mate. 'You gotta listen to her, Buk. She don't take no for an answer, see. And she's got a bigger gun than you.'

'Geez... I didn't sign up for making decisions, man.'

'Then I'll make it. You open them gates, and keep 'em open 'til we leave, ok? Otherwise I'll just shoot them apart, you understand what I'm saying?'

Sarah glared at him.

'What?'

Before she had chance to say anything, she was forced to accept Wilfred knew how to talk to his mates better than she did. Buk nodded reluctantly, and pressed the keypad on his arm. The heavy gates started to swing open. Sarah smiled to Will, acknowledging the fact she was more grateful than ever to have him as a deputy.

'See boss? Now just admit you can't do without me.'

'Ok... I can't do without you. Happy now?'

'Sure as hell am,' he grinned, and then called out to his friend as the Nissan moved away. 'And don't you go telling no one we's coming, ok Buk? This is a surprise gate-crashing!'

Wilfred drove slowly up the slightly-sloping drive. Thirty feet from the oversized porch he turned off the engine, and the minibus rolled to an almost-silent stop just before the main entrance doors.

'You done this before?' said Sarah curiously.

'Hey boss, that ain't for your ears. Just think on, life was hard in Kampala if you wasn't privileged. I ain't always been an honest taxi driver. You giving me that rifle?'

Sarah handed it over, and swallowed hard. There was nothing they could see through the brightly-lit windows to indicate Daisy and Aidan were in danger. Neither was there anything to indicate they weren't.

Or even if they were still there. The innocent-looking façade gave nothing away, but something was telling her all was not as peaceful as it seemed. She looked pointedly at Will.

'Ok, deputy... you know what we've got to do?'

He gripped the rifle a little more firmly, and narrowed he is eyes. 'Sure thing, boss. Let's do it.'

They slipped quietly out of the minibus. Sarah could feel her heart thumping in her chest like a rubber ball that wouldn't stop bouncing. If her friends' lives were in jeopardy, the only people who could save them now were a rookie British cop, and a teenage Ugandan taxi driver brandishing a Russian automatic rifle.

But, as the increasingly-loud voice in her head kept telling her, it was all she had.

Chapter 27

The four guards with the blank expressions began to move towards Daisy and Aidan. Then they hesitated. They could all hear some sort of disturbance, out in the entrance hall. Seconds later the housekeeper threw open the study door, her face clouded with petrified apology.

'I'm so sorry, General...'

She didn't get chance to say anything else. Two people brushed past her, one brandishing a police badge, one brandishing an automatic rifle.

'Stick 'em up!' shouted Will.

'What?' said Sarah, glaring disbelievingly at him.

'Ok... um, *hands on your head!'*

'What is this?' asked a rather-shocked General Oyite.

'Wilfred?' gasped a very shocked Daisy.

Sarah strode into the room, as Will flicked the barrel of his gun from one guard to the other, all four of whom were looking more than a little bemused.

'I do apologise for the intrusion, General Oyite. I'm Officer Sarah Lowry of the British secret police...'

'You... you are?'

'I'm here to arrest these two people under the Terrorist Extortion Act, two-thousand-and-eighteen. You were in danger of becoming one of their victims, general.'

'I was?'

'Yes, sir. I've been chasing these... criminals for a while now. They operate by accusing innocent high-ranking officials of serious crimes, saying they have irrefutable proof of wrongdoing, and then demanding money for keeping quiet. You were lucky, general... we had been tracking them to this location.'

'You had?' said the general.

'You had?' said Daisy, genuinely surprised by what she was hearing.

Aidan, realising they had to play the game, raised his hands above his head. 'It's a fair cop, Miss,' he said.

'*Seriously?*' said Daisy, looking disbelievingly at Aidan.

Sarah wasn't taking prisoners. Well, she was, in one sense. She beckoned to Will to train the gun on the perpetrators. 'Come along, you two. You're under arrest. Anything you say may be used against you in a court of law. Do you understand?'

'Um... I think so...' said Daisy.

'*Out*... we're taking you back to England to stand trial.'

The grinning Will stuck the barrel of the gun into Aidan's back, but only gently. 'Make a run for it and I'll shoot you,' he growled, as menacingly as he could.

'Oh dear,' said Daisy, as they were shepherded through the study door and led across the white tiles of the entrance hall floor. She glanced back as they walked, and noticed the general emerge from the study, shaking his head in a slightly-unconvinced way.

'Oh dear,' she said again, almost to herself.

Sarah was still taking prisoners, marching her two perpetrators to the minibus, making sure they sat in the back seat by putting a hand on their heads, as all the best cops do. Then she took the rifle from Will's hands, flicked it momentarily at the two criminals in the back seat, and then barked out an instruction to her deputy as she climbed into the front seat.

'*Drive!*'

Only too keen to oblige, Will floored the throttle and the Nissan screeched around the circular drive towards the rear gate.

'It's a fair cop, guv'nor?' Daisy glared to Aidan.

'To be fair, I didn't say guv'nor. But in any case, we've just got away with our lives, and that's all you can say?'

'Terrorist Extortion act?' Daisy flicked the glare to Sarah instead.

'I thought it was quite clever,' she pouted.

'And British secret police? Have we travelled back to World War Two now?'

'I didn't want to say I worked for a real department, just in case.'

Daisy shook her head, knowing if the roles had been reversed she would likely have said something similar. 'I was just about to look for Celia.'

'No you weren't, dear,' said Aidan. 'You were about to be taken on a drive to oblivion, along with me.'

'Well, I *wanted* to look for Celia.'

'Not exactly the relevant point, Petal. Thank you for intervening, Sarah.'

'That's not a problem. At least *one* of you is grateful.'

'Oh Sarah dear, I'm indebted to you. Things were going exactly as I'd anticipated, except for the four armed guards, who might have ruined everything.'

'Did it work?' asked Aidan.

Daisy pulled the phone from her pocket, and grinned. 'Still recording, so we should have every word of that conversation on record.'

She switched off the microphone, as Will screeched to a stop outside the little guard hut. *'Buk... get in, quick!'*

The young guard looked just as bemused as everyone else. 'Will... I got a job to do, man.'

145

'No you ain't, mate. Not anymore. This whole thing gonna blow sky high, so you's better come with us, while you still can.'

'Aw, hell man...'

He jumped into the rear seat, and the minibus squealed a left, and headed down Kololo Hill Drive.

Daisy glanced back along the moonlit road, and her heart sank through the slightly-rusty floor. 'Yes, I thought so.'

'Dear?'

'Whatever the hell you're doing here Wilfred, I suggest you put your foot down... as far as it will go, anyway.'

'Huh?'

'There's an open Landrover just steamed out of the general's drive, with a small army of his loyal troops in the back. I don't think he bought your sting after all, Sarah.'

Chapter 28

Will, still grinning from ear to ear, did as he was asked. Unfortunately the ancient Nissan had seen better days, and was no match for the much-newer Landrover. Within a half-mile, its headlights were filling the rear view mirror.

'Give me the rifle,' cried Daisy.

'Daisy?' said Sarah, handing it back to her anyway.

'My turn now,' she grinned, flicking off the safety catch and winding down the rear window.

'You can't go playing Bonnie Parker in the middle of Kololo...' gasped Aidan.

'Oh, do be quiet, Clyde. You want the cops to catch us, or not?'

'I seem to recall things didn't end too well for them either.'

Buk, seeing what Daisy was about to do, and still holding his army-issued rifle, wound down his window too. They both turned, pointed their weapons backwards at the chasing troops.

'*Shoot the tyres out,*' shouted Daisy to him. 'It won't go down too well if we kill someone.'

The Nissan had just careered past the primary school. Then they were speeding through a more commercial part of Kololo. It was gone eleven, and no one was about.

'*Now!*'

A hail of gangster-style fire-power streaked out from both sides of the minibus. The Landrover, less than a hundred yards behind, was an easy target for an ex-secret agent and a trained army private.

The driver slewed to the opposite side of the road, and then back again. Someone in the back started firing, but he only managed to let off a few rounds before both front tyres blew, and the vehicle slewed again.

This time there was no way it was going to keep in a straight line. As everyone in the minibus watched in horror, it left the road and smashed into a tree trunk in a wooded part of the roadside, coming to an abrupt halt in a cloud of radiator steam.

It didn't look like anyone was seriously hurt; the occupants were too busy jumping out, gesticulating their emotions furiously. As the Nissan raced away into the distance, there was nothing the troops could do except watch it dwindle to a speck, and then slink back on foot and report to their general they'd lost their target... and wrecked a Landrover into the bargain.

The Nissan drove along Kintu Road, a little more serenely. Outside the hotel, the muzungus climbed out. Daisy, still looking a little curious, smiled to Will. 'I still have no idea how you became a deputy of the British police, but thank you for your help. And you too, Buk. I'm sorry about your job. But I'm concerned about you both. Will you be okay?'

Will had a serious look on his face, for once. 'Sure, Mrs. Henderson. Buk is coming home with me. No one knows where I live. We'll lay low for a while, until that general gets his come-uppance... whatever he's done.'

'He's a murderous thug, Will,' said Aidan. 'But you've helped make it possible to bring him down. Thank you both.' He held out a hand, which they both shook.

Daisy, Aidan and Sarah started to walk towards the hotel. Will called to Sarah. 'Hey, Sarah? You got a sec?'

148

She came back to the driver's door. 'You did good Will, but there still isn't time for you to... show me the sights. This isn't over yet.'

'Nah, that wasn't what I was going to say. That stuff about Celia... what's that all about?'

She hesitated, unsure if Daisy would want it to be common knowledge. Then she shook her head. Will and his mate had made it possible for them to stay alive, so they deserved to know. 'Keep it to yourselves, guys, but the real reason we came to Uganda was to find their daughter. She was trafficked three years ago, and it turns out the general bought her... at least it looks like he did. We all came to get her back, which was what tonight was about, until you and me gate-crashed the party. So now you know.'

'Geez, that guy has some stuff to answer for. But their daughter, she must be getting on a bit, judging by Daisy and Aidan being ol... senior citizens, I mean.'

Sarah shook her head. 'She's only a little older than me. They had her quite late in life, apparently. She looks a bit like me too.'

Will glanced to Buk, and then gave Sarah a big grin. 'Ok, girl. See ya around, maybe... boss.'

The minibus drove away, and Sarah joined Daisy and Aidan, waiting for her at the entrance door.

The ground floor was deserted. Not that many guests were staying in the hotel anyway, with no conferences on right then. They smiled sweetly to the night porter, and slipped into the elevator to the eighth floor.

Back in their rooms, Daisy pulled the rifle from the sports bag. 'Guys, it might be prudent to get out of this place, but we can't do it until morning without raising suspicion.'

'I guess the general won't be too pleased about tonight.'

149

'That's an understatement. He might not know where we're staying though.'

'You *really* think he can't find out?'

'Not for a minute. Which is why you and me are taking it in turns to keep watch until morning, and then we'll check out.'

'What about me?' said Sarah.

'Go get some sleep. You'll be fine, no one in authority here sees you as a threat. Just keep your door latched, ok? And your phone by the bedside.'

'If you're sure. I called Anton earlier; he's worried about you, said he'd be here in the morning to do what he could.'

'Good. He can help us find somewhere to stay, out of sight. Plus, I think we've got enough now to officially incriminate Emmanuel Oyite, don't you Dip? We'll give it all to Anton, and he can use his status to let the British ambassador know what we've unearthed. He should be able to make things happen.'

He nodded his head. 'Yes. But the general is probably aware he's incriminated himself.'

'Which is why we need to stay awake tonight. Two-hour stints, ok?'

Aidan got himself ready for bed. As he padded back from the en suite, he caught sight of Daisy leaning on the balcony rail. He went to join her, wrapped his arms around her and held her tight to him. He could see the tears in her eyes as she whispered quietly.

'We made a bit of an impression over there tonight, dear.'

'We did, and I fear the general won't take it lying down.'

'And still we haven't rescued Celia.'

150

'But we've got what we need now to expose him. The authorities will find her for us.'

She turned to him, and he felt her body shaking against his. 'Will they? If she's his star prize and he realises his world is falling apart, he might disappear and take her with him. Or even... he might...'

Aidan knew she was right, but also knew he had to keep her in one piece. 'He believes he's untouchable, remember? I doubt he will run away from all he possesses until he knows for sure he's *not* untouchable.'

'And as soon as we pass everything on to Anton and he does his stuff, things might happen quickly. We're running out of time to get our daughter back, Dip.'

'Perhaps. But we have to wait until Anton gets here in the morning. He knows a lot more about how things work around here than we do. We might have to be guided by him.'

Daisy pulled away, leant on the rail again and gazed out at Kololo like it was Hell on Earth. 'I know, dear. But what he has to do officially might actually be more of a hindrance to our personal quest. Somehow we have to get Celia out of there before the shit hits the fan.'

He saw her head lower, pulled her into him and wiped away her tears with his fingers. 'Then when we bring Anton up to speed, we have to tell him that too. We all make a plan, together, ok?'

She nodded desolately. 'Go get your two hours, dear. I'll keep watch, and then it's your turn.'

'I'm not sure I'll sleep, exhausted though I am.'

'Just try, Dip. I need you refreshed, so you can hold me up.'

Chapter 29

Daisy sat quietly on the sofa in the room, her phone by her side, the automatic rifle cradled in her arms. It was just gone midnight, and after a few half-slurred words Aidan had fallen asleep, much to her relief.

All seemed peaceful. She'd left all three table lamps burning, as much for her own peace of mind as to actually see anything. A dull ache of dread growled constantly in her stomach, and she knew she was clock-watching; not until it was time to wake Aidan for his watch, but until it was time when they could pack their bags and leave the hotel that right then felt like their prison.

She knew the general couldn't afford to ignore the fact they'd forced his hand. Apart from getting Celia back, it had been the plan to make him try something that would finally implicate him. Sarah interfering had likely saved their lives back at his house, but they were hardly out of danger. It wouldn't be difficult for a man in the general's position to find out where they were staying.

And it wouldn't be hard for him to issue orders to his loyal troops, and make sure they didn't get the opportunity to bring his world crashing down.

Her thoughts turned to Celia. They hadn't set eyes on her at the general's house, and they still didn't know for sure it was he who'd got her. But somehow her gut knew for sure. He'd denied it of course, but that was to be expected.

She wondered what kind of treatment Celia was receiving. Like her mother, she wasn't one for doing anything she didn't want to do. For three years she'd been at the general's mercy, but she wouldn't have done so willingly. Somehow he'd managed to keep her tamed. He'd all but admitted he had a thing for white women, but Daisy couldn't imagine he would have the patience to spend too long turning Celia into a willing captive.

She let out a little cry, as one horrific scenario hit home.

If he hadn't managed to turn her into a submissive pussycat, not an easy task where Celia was concerned, he might have lost patience. Celia might not even exist anymore, because he sure wouldn't just simply let her go. Not alive.

She wiped away a tear, tried to pull herself together. It was also a possibility Celia had realised playing the submissive was a way to buy time until she could escape.

But that was three years ago.

She forced herself to rip the depressing thoughts away, glanced at her watch. It was about time to wake Aidan for his stint. She dragged her weary body over to the kettle, flicked it on to make them both a coffee. He would need one, just to stay awake if nothing else.

A half-hour later he gave her a hug, and tucked her up in the bed like a little child. She told him she loved him, and that she wasn't expecting to find sleep.

'Would you like a bedtime story, dear?' he grinned.

'I think I've heard enough stories in the last few days to last me a lifetime, thanks all the same.'

He nodded his head, ordered her to sleep, and told her he wouldn't let go of the rifle, even though he'd never actually fired a gun in his life.

He settled onto the sofa, opened the laptop and copied Daisy's phone recording of their conversation with the general, listening to it through the headphones as he did. It was a little muffled, but legible. It didn't make easy listening, and he knew it wouldn't stand up in an English court of law.

But for the high-ranking general it was yet more incriminating evidence, which the British consulate could not ignore when British citizens were involved. The highest levels of Ugandan hierarchy could not ignore it either, if they wished to avoid an international incident.

Whether the general would actually be prosecuted was another matter... but he would for sure be exiled, and live out the remainder of his life in a manner to which he certainly wasn't accustomed.

But it was risky to have only one copy of the phone recording. The general didn't know Daisy had made it, but if he ordered someone to come and shut them up that night, they would for sure also have been told to take their phones and laptop.

He wrote a quick mail to Anton, and sent him a copy of the recording.

Then there *wasn't* just one copy.

An hour later he was standing on the balcony, gazing down to the silent, still-illuminated swimming pool a few stories below, and then lifting his eyes to peer over to Kololo Hill. He wondered to himself, as Daisy had done, if Celia was there, living a new life that had been forced upon her, oblivious to the fact her parents had been just metres away from her a few hours ago.

He shook his head, tried not to think about what his daughter had gone through, and wished her a peaceful night's sleep.

It was almost time to wake Daisy. He did as she had done, flicked on the kettle, and made her a mega-strong brew to help keep her awake for her last stint of the night.

154

It was four in the morning, and in two hours would be getting light... if the general's men hadn't come by then, they might just have made it through the night, and be able to slip away unhindered.

Daisy looked grateful for the coffee, and they took five minutes to sit side by side in the bed, sipping the brew. He told her what he'd done with the recording, and then she slipped out of bed and kissed him softly, turned his order on its head and reminded him it was his turn to catch some sleep, or else.

She watched him as he fell asleep, and then settled back on the sofa. Two hours sleep had been welcome, but not really enough. She's spent much of the day running on adrenaline, and finally being able to cool off, that was mentally exhausting on its own.

She hit the kettle again, made a stand-the-spoon-up-in-it brew, knowing she dare not fall asleep, just in case they did get a visitation.

Four-thirty. It was beginning to look like they might get away with it after all. Everything was quiet, the almost-imperceptible hum of the air-conditioners the only sound. Once they checked out of the hotel in a couple of hours, the general would never find them, especially with Anton's help. Once the daylight came, it would just be a case of a quick pack, saying a hasty goodbye to the receptionist, and then waiting in a quiet cafe somewhere for Anton to join them.

Then they would have to decide on a plan to extract Celia from her luxury jail, before the general did something they all regretted.

She rested her head against the back of the sofa, starting to feel they might just get through the night after all. Then she realised she was relaxing just a little too much, and her eyes had closed. Just before she drifted away, she gave herself a mental slap.

Wide awake again, she did all she could to stop her eyes closing once more. It wasn't enough. Her head sank forward, the need for sleep overpowering the need to stay awake. She didn't even realise she'd drifted away, until her chin dropped onto her chest and she jerked herself awake again.

Just in time to see two shadowy dark figures climbing onto the balcony.

Chapter 30

Daisy blinked away the almost-sleep. For a moment she thought she might be dreaming, but as her hands tightened automatically around the rifle, somehow she knew it was a nightmare, but not one brought about by her subconscious.

But in the few moments it took her to work out it was all too real, the two figures dressed in black were already in the room.

'Dip,' she hissed, struggling to her feet as Aidan woke in an instant, sitting up on his elbows. She raised the gun to her shoulder, spotted the vicious-looking blade of a knife in the hand of one of the men as it glinted in the lamplight.

She also saw the shocked expressions of the two Ugandan men, as they realised their quarry wasn't the pushover they thought. An elderly muzungu brandishing an automatic rifle in their direction was the last thing they expected to see.

They glanced to each other, but in the second or two it took to hesitate, a flying pillow crashed into one of them.

'Take that!' said Aidan, using the only weapon he had at his disposal to try and make an impression. Daisy, using the distraction to wrench herself fully-awake, made a deliberately-dramatic meal of flicking off the rifle's safety catch.

'I don't want to kill you, but I sure as hell will if I have to,' she growled.

The two thugs looked at each other again. Faced with an automatic rifle on one flank, and a second pillow in the hand of a determined opponent on the other, things weren't looking so good.

One of them decided he'd had enough. He bolted for his life, made a run for the door. He reached out for the handle, but Aidan and the lethal pillow were right behind him. He raised the fluffy weapon, but the guy still had the knife in his hand, and lashed out backwards.

The casing of the pillow split open, a shower of duck-feathers flying everywhere. For a moment Aidan couldn't see a thing, and in the three seconds it took to bat away the feathery cloud, the guy was through the door.

Running straight into a panicking Sarah.

Literally. Her slim frame was no match for a six-foot ballistic missile, and she crashed to the floor of the open walkway as the thug skittled her, luckily without the time or the thought to bring the knife into play. Sarah scrambled to her feet as her personal bowling ball ran for the stairs, sucked in a deep breath and started to go after the man. Aidan pulled her back. *'Leave it, Sarah,'* he cried. 'He's gone. And there's another one in the room anyway.'

The other thug had raised his hands. A rifle was belted behind his shoulder, but he knew he had no chance of getting to it before finding out someone else's bullet had his name on it. His eyes were big and wide, his head flicking from side to side as the realisation rammed home the mission he'd been given was about to become a dismal, unforgiving failure.

'Give me your gun...' Daisy growled.

Still his big eyes were searching for some kind of divine intervention that was never going to come. Daisy could see all too well the panic written across his face. It was clear going back to the general to report yet another fail wasn't going to be so good for his army career. And that fact alone meant his next move was as unpredictable as it gets.

158

'Hey, look at me. I'm not going to harm you... as long as you come clean, and tell us who gave you the orders.' Daisy tried to say the right words to calm him down, although the right words weren't too obvious at that moment. And given the *out of the frying pan into the fire* scenario that had just presented itself to the man, the right words didn't really exist.

The thug seemed to agree with that. He bolted too, deciding last-chance-saloon was the only option left. Aidan and Sarah were standing in the doorway to the walkway, both of them watching his every move with angry eyes. Getting out that way wasn't the best idea. His only route was the way he'd arrived.

He streaked through the open balcony doors. Aidan saw Daisy raise the rifle again, put a hand on the barrel and shoved it back down. 'Dear, you can't... not here...'

She knew he was right, and reluctantly shook her head. As the three of them ran to the balcony after the guy, he was already climbing over the edge of the rail, his hand reaching for the rope still hanging there, tied to a grappling-hook.

'Hey... get back here...'

Aidan's shout made him glance up. Whether the shout broke his concentration, or he was just too far into panic mode, they would never know. But as he dropped below the balcony rail in desperation to get away, his hand missed the rope.

They heard the sickening crunch as he hit the extended roof of the balcony below, and the three of them reached their balcony rail in time to see him belly-flop into the deserted swimming pool several stories below.

'Oh dear,' said Daisy, as the huge splash resonated around the poolside walls.

'Did I do that?' said Aidan.

'We all did it, dear. And now we have to pretend we didn't.' She unhooked both the grappling-hooks, threw them down to the pool after the thug. 'Close the door, quick. The night porter must have seen the second thug running out through the main entrance, but he won't know which room he came from.'

Sarah peeped out onto the walkway. No one seemed to be around. Luckily, hardly any guests were staying on the eighth floor. She closed the door to the room quietly, sucked in a deep breath.

'Everyone ok?' she asked.

Daisy was peeping over the balcony rail to the scene below. A couple of the night staff were at the poolside, fishing the man from the pool. It wasn't clear if he was dead, or just unconscious. But he'd had a pretty eventful trip in a downwards direction, so he sure wasn't going to be very well.

Aidan slumped onto the bed. 'I'm ok. That knife missed my hands by inches. The pillow got it though.' He brushed away a couple of feathers as he spoke.

Daisy closed the balcony doors. 'Never knew you were so handy with soft furnishings, Dip.'

He found a grin. 'Comes of dormitory pillow fights, back at boarding school.'

She sat down beside him. 'Thank you, dear. That missile made them think twice.'

'I think it might have had something to do with the automatic rifle they weren't expecting as well.'

'Maybe. But now I suggest we get into bed, and pretend like nothing happened. It's getting light. How about we snuggle up for an hour, just in case someone comes wondering if we were involved, and then pack our stuff and get out of here?'

Sarah nodded her head. 'It will look as suspicious as hell if we clear off right now.'

'Exactly. We need to make it look like we're checking out *because* of the night-time disturbances, not that we were the cause of them,' Aidan agreed.

'Sarah, there won't be any trouble now, the sun is coming up. Sneak back to your room, give it a good hour, and then pack your stuff.'

She nodded, and slipped away without a word. Aidan flicked on the kettle. 'Nuclear-level coffee, dear?'

'Got any brandy?'

He opened a drawer below the kettle, pulled out the bottle. 'Coming right up.'

Daisy set the alarm for six-thirty, and slipped into bed. 'Let's pretend to sleep, dear. Oh, you'd better get another pillow from the wardrobe!'

Chapter 31

'Do you think the guy who ran away has reported back?' asked Aidan as he stuffed a few things into the case.

'I doubt it. Knowing the general, he'll probably be shot at dawn for failing in his duties. He's likely a long way from here now.'

'What about the diving guy?'

'I don't know. If he's not dead he'll be in the hospital.'

Daisy stopped packing, snuck another peek over the balcony rail. There was no sign anyone had taken an unintentional high-dive; the swimming pool looked just like it was ready to take the day's recreational swimmers.

'Nothing to see there, dear. We almost ready to make our escape?'

He closed the lid on the case, nodded nervously. Daisy called Sarah on her phone. 'You ready?'

She said she was, and two minutes later there was a tap on the door. Aidan let her in, saw the equally-nervous look on her face. 'Don't panic, Sarah. We're really just checking out early, after all.'

She nodded, didn't say a word.

It was seven in the morning. Still too early for most guests to be up and about, but plenty late enough for people who were actually fleeing the scene of the crime to be appearing like they were simply checking out. Aidan grabbed their luggage, and they strolled out onto the walkway, trying not to look too furtive.

'Ok, best dissatisfied faces,' said Daisy as the elevator doors slid aside, and the deserted ground floor came into view. She marched across the vast space, right up to the reception desk. A young receptionist had already taken over from the night porter.

'I really must complain, dear. We've hardly had a decent night's sleep since we've been here. And after that disturbance last night, we've decided we'd like to check out, please.'

She didn't exactly look surprised. 'I'm so sorry, Mrs. Henderson. I can assure you incidences like you witnessed last night are extremely rare. Can I give you my sincere apologies?'

'You can, but it won't make any difference. We have booked into the Sheraton for the remainder of our stay. And I think as a mark of respect, you should waive any additional charges we have clocked up.'

'Oh... I don't think the manager would allow that, Mrs. Henderson.'

'Really? So when I post my review on Tripadvisor, and tell them how disgusted we are, and then inform the press that criminals apparently see this hotel as a rich picking ground, he's going to be happy?'

'I... um... perhaps I can remove any extra charges without him knowing.'

'I should think so. It's a disgrace. And there's a crack in the ceiling!'

Aidan handed back the room keys, and Sarah did the same. All three of them were watching the receptionist as she printed off the checkout receipt. None of them noticed the six men who had just marched through the entrance doors, until one of them spoke. It was a voice they'd heard once before.

'Mr. and Mrs. Henderson. Do I presume you are going somewhere?'

163

Daisy spun round, a big beaming smile on her face she certainly didn't feel like smiling. 'Ah, Inspector General. We are indeed honoured, yet again. What brings you here so early in the morning?'

He growled out the words, even more menacingly than usual. 'It has distressed me more than I care to think about that I have been dragged from my bed at such an ungodly hour. But sadly, urgent matters have dictated that I was.'

'Yes, indeed. Whatever happened last night has distressed us too. We came here for a relaxing holiday, and last night was the final straw. We did not realise thieves frequented this establishment so much, Inspector General.'

'*Thieves*, Mrs. Henderson?'

'Indeed. We do not have flights home for another week, but we've decided to change hotels for the rest of our stay, in the hope we shall receive a better, safer experience.'

'Really?'

'Do you not think you... need to clean up your act in Kampala, Mr. Osambu?'

'To be honest, Mrs. Henderson, that is why I have been dragged from my bed.'

Daisy felt the all-too-familiar thump of dread churn her stomach inside out, but forced herself to keep the slightly distasteful smile on her face. 'Glad to hear it. You really need to get on top of things, you know.'

'Trust me, I intend to. Starting with the fact that from the first hour you were in Uganda, it seems death and other incidents have been your constant companions.'

Daisy tried to look shocked. 'Oh, Inspector General... can I help it if one of your citizens dies at my feet as soon as we get here?'

'I do not know, Mrs. Henderson. Can you?'

164

She threw hands to her face, trying to appear even more shocked. '*Oh my goodness*... are you saying we had something to do with his death?'

He shook his head. The five armed policemen just behind him moved forward a step or two. It was starting to look like he may believe they had something to do with it after all.

'In truth, I do not know. But as there seems to have been several incidents involving you since that day, I am not prepared to take the chance of your innocence, Mr. and Mrs. Henderson.'

'What... what are you saying?' Daisy stuttered, genuinely this time. 'We're just transferring to the Sheraton, we don't wish for any more trouble.'

'Unfortunately, the Sheraton will not solve the problem.'

Aidan stepped forward, even though he knew it was futile. 'Are you threatening us, sir?'

'No, Mr. Henderson. I am arresting you.'

'Oh really... we're citizens of the United Kingdom, Inspector General,' Daisy protested, knowing just as Aidan did the words were pointless.

The officers stepped forward, spun the three of them around and wrenched their hands behind their backs. The click of locking handcuffs filled their ears.

'I really must protest...' said Daisy, in a small voice she just couldn't make any bigger.

The Inspector General put his face next to hers. 'Perhaps you should see it as something for your own protection, Mrs. Henderson. Or perhaps, for the protection of Uganda.'

'Well, that's comforting.'

Martin Osamba clicked his fingers at his officers, and Daisy, Aidan and Sarah were led away from the reception desk. They only got a few steps before the entrance door burst open, and someone else arrived.

'*Stop!*' he shouted out, his single word reverberating around the vast empty space.

Chapter 32

'Release these people, Inspector General. They have diplomatic Immunity!'

The chief of police looked at the man in the suit open-mouthed. 'I beg your pardon?'

The man fumbled in the briefcase he was holding, handed over three pieces of paper. 'Miss Lowry is an officer of the British police, involved in a covert mission. Mr. and Mrs. Henderson are British Intelligence, accompanying her here on a matter of international importance.'

The Inspector General scanned the official-looking papers, shook his head in a slightly disbelieving way, and then glanced up, still a little open-mouthed. 'And you are?'

'Anton Kowalski, American embassy. As you can see, arresting them will cause a serious international incident between our nations.'

'I… this is somewhat unexpected.'

'It was necessary for them to remain incognito. So now you are aware of their status, please remove the handcuffs.'

The Inspector General nodded to his officers, who did as Anton asked. The embassy official snatched back the papers. 'In the circumstances, I cannot allow these papers to leave my possession. I hope you understand, sir. And I must ask you not to speak of this to anyone. Their mission is not yet complete, and if it becomes common knowledge, will be compromised. Do you understand, Inspector General?'

He nodded dumbly, more than a little bemused. Anton looked pointedly at Daisy. 'Please, you three, come with me. The ambassador needs to be briefed on your progress.'

Daisy, Aidan and Sarah picked up their luggage, and smiled sweetly to the officers as Anton led the way to the exit door. Daisy grinned to him.

'This is the second time you've saved my life.'

'Just keep quiet, until we're away from here.'

'Diplomatic immunity?' Daisy asked incredulously as they piled quickly into the Volkswagen minibus on the hotel forecourt.

Anton dropped into the driving seat, floored the throttle. 'Cool, huh? I sorted it out before I left the embassy, just in case it was needed. I know you, remember?' he grinned.

'But... the papers?'

'Typed them myself, on embassy headed notepaper. But he's no fool; as soon as he checks he'll realise it was a scam. But it got you out of there.'

'Thank you, my friend. What's with the suit and tie?'

'Quite honestly it's driving me nuts. But I guessed, correctly, it might give me more kudos than looking like a hillbilly.'

'What now, Anton?'

'We gotta get you to the British embassy, for your own protection. It'll be fine, the British ambassador is a friend of mine. I've got all the evidence here on the laptop, so when we hand it over he'll do what needs to be done.'

Aidan called out from the rear seat. 'How quickly will he act, Anton?'

'Folks, you gotta realise how things work around here. If we ask him nicely, it'll happen today. Those in positions of power here tend to disappear very quickly when they realise they need to.'

Daisy lowered her head. 'That's what I'm afraid of, Anton. The general is no fool either, and when he gets wind of trouble he can't make go away, he'll clear off and likely take Celia with him.'

'Geez, I hadn't thought of that. These top military types always seem to have a back door. But we gotta let the embassy have what we've got, and quick, Daisy.'

'I know. But the three of us came to rescue Celia before other things happened around us. As you said to the Inspector General, we still haven't completed our mission. And if the general buggers off to Rwanda or somewhere, we never will.'

He glanced across, saw the mistiness in her eyes. 'Ok. So what do you suggest?'

Daisy looked round to Aidan and Sarah, who lifted her eyes to the van roof. 'We know where he lives, at the moment anyway,' she said, in a resigned kind of way.

Aidan said nothing, but the telepathic look he gave Daisy didn't need words.

She turned back to Anton. 'My dear friend, I know you won't like this, but I want you to do what you said, take all the evidence to the British ambassador, and also tell him the general bought a trafficked British girl three years ago.'

'So what's not to like?'

'The next bit. We need you to pretend you've not seen us today. While you're telling the ambassador everything, we have to go and rescue Celia. Somehow.'

'You're right about me not liking it, girl. I never was too hot on suicide missions. The general probably won't know yet the shit is about to hit the fan, so he'll still be keen to stop it happening. By making it so you stop living. And you're just gonna walk in there like you *want* to stop living?'

Daisy wiped away a tear. 'Anton, I know Celia is at his home. Don't ask me how, I just do. But in order to get justice for Joseph and Florence, and make it so Michael didn't lose his life in vain, you've got to do your thing and let the powers-that-be know what's what. And you must do it in the next couple of hours, before the big police gun works out he's been duped and you get arrested.'

'And what about you three?'

'Somehow, before it all blows up in everybody's face, we've got to rescue Celia.'

Chapter 33

Anton drove into the car park of the British embassy, turned off the Volkswagen's engine and turned to Daisy.

'I ain't happy about this, Petal.'

'You think we are?'

'That's not what I meant. You should let the authorities deal with it now.'

She sighed, a little louder than necessary so she could make a point. 'We've been over this, Anton. There's no guarantee the authorities will do the right thing, and even if they do the right thing, the general will know his world is about to come crashing down. So are you telling me you can't predict what his next move will be?'

He shook his head. 'Ok, you got me, as usual. I live in Africa, so it ain't difficult to see he'll use his secret exit route and disappear over the border.'

'And very likely take his prize possession with him. So now give us this bus please, and pretend you never saw us. Call me when you're done, and we'll come and pick you up.'

'Just make sure you *can* come and pick me up, deal?'

'Deal. Now bugger off and do what you've got to.'

He shook his head, knowing Daisy was going to attempt the impossible no matter what he said. He climbed out of the bus, and Daisy handed him the briefcase with the laptop inside it. He leant back through the open window. 'Just don't bend this bus… it's a hire car I picked up at the airport. Taking it back with bullet holes in the bodywork is a dead cert I'll lose my deposit!'

Daisy grinned, watched him walk into the building, and then turned to Sarah. 'Will you drive, dear? You're the only one of us with a police badge, so if we get stopped it might come in handy.'

Sarah shook her head, and sank into the driver's seat. Daisy joined Aidan in the rear seat, wrapped her hand around his. 'It'll be fine, dear, you'll see.'

With Sarah at the wheel, the bus headed along the Jinja highway, and then turned left in the direction of Kololo. Then, as they reached the golf course, something caught her eye. 'There's a huge pall of smoke coming from somewhere further up the hill, guys. Something's well alight.'

Daisy tried to see where it was coming from, but still a distance away, it was impossible to know. It didn't stop her glancing to Aidan though, and squeezing his hand a little harder. Then Sarah slowed and pulled to the verge, as a fire truck raced past them, blue lights flashing, its headlights blinking a warning to the morning traffic to get out of the way.

Thirty seconds later it was followed by a second truck, careering a slightly-snaking path up Kololo Hill. Sarah floored the throttle again. 'I hope they haven't closed a road. It might make getting to the general's house a bit harder,' she said.

Daisy glanced to Aidan again, but didn't say anything. The look on her face kind of said it all. As the bus turned into Kololo Hill Drive, the pall of heavy smoke looked like a fog. Sarah was the first to say something.

'Oh my god...'

Daisy followed that up with a little more detail. 'I think it's coming from the general's house,' she whispered.

'We can't really tell from here, all these trees in the way,' said the ever-optimistic Aidan.

Two army trucks were parked across the road, forming a blockade. Sarah braked to a halt, two hundred yards before the short drive to the fortified concrete walls of the compound. Twelve feet high or not, they couldn't hide the flames searing into the sky from somewhere inside them.

'Oh no...' cried Daisy. 'Celia...'

The road just outside the general's residence was a mass of activity. Police vehicles, army trucks and one of the fire trucks that had arrived too late were parked between the crowds of onlookers, who were standing around with shocked expressions on their faces. It wasn't possible to make out too much beyond the trucks blocking the road and their line of sight, but what they could see painted a horrific picture.

The general's house was well ablaze.

Sarah wound the window down as an army officer walked over to them. 'Sorry, there's no way through. You'll have to go back, find another route.'

She flashed her badge quickly. 'Sir, I'm Officer Lowry, police. We were heading to the general's house. What's happened?'

He glanced over his shoulder. 'As you can see, officer, the house is burning to the ground. We don't yet know if there are any casualties, but the fire is so fierce the fire service is not equipped to put it out. It looks like all they can do is prevent it spreading to other properties.'

'Sarah...' Daisy let out a strangled plea.

She knew exactly what Daisy was trying to say. 'Please let me through, sir. I need to have a closer look. It's an ongoing police investigation.'

The army man looked uncomfortable, unsure what he should do. He glanced to the rear seat. 'Are those people civilians, officer?'

173

'Yes, but I'm not.'

'You can't drive any further, but I will let just you through on foot. But not beyond the gates. Please stay on the road outside.'

Sarah nodded, as the sergeant walked back to his blockade. 'I'll go see what I can find out, guys. Please stay here, Daisy. I won't be long.'

Daisy nodded dumbly, and watched through misty eyes as Sarah disappeared behind the army truck. Then she looked at Aidan. 'He's torched his own place, hasn't he? The piece of shit has made a run for it, and...'

The words died away into a sob, as she buried her face into Aidan's shoulder and felt his gentle arms close around her. 'If he has, Flower, he might have taken Celia with him.'

'You think?'

He couldn't reply. It was just as possible he'd decided everything he possessed was never going to be owned by anyone else.

Everything.

Sarah found a crowd of shell-shocked people standing around looking like they couldn't believe what was happening. Most of them who weren't just onlookers appeared to be the general's security guards, their weapons slung over their shoulders.

Two or three were women. White women. As her heart missed a beat she moved a little closer. She recognised Alice, the housekeeper. Two other white girls seemed to be wearing service uniforms.

Neither of them was Celia.

She walked closer to the open gates, but then a fire officer pulled her back. 'Miss, you can't go in there. It's an inferno.'

174

'I'm looking for someone…'

'Sorry. If anyone is still in there, they don't stand a chance now.'

She tried to break free, but his grip was firm. '*Look…*' she growled, flashing her badge at him for a fleeting second. 'I'm police. You don't have…'

'Sorry, miss. Where life-threatening fire is concerned, I do have authority. No one is getting in there now.'

She cried out her frustration and anger, but knew he was right. Through the open gates she could see trees ablaze, and the red mist of the inferno smoking everything out. And as she watched, the first fire truck backed out onto the short drive, the young fire-fighters aiming a weak spray of water over the top of the wall.

Even the fire department had retreated.

She pushed her way through the crowd of people, making absolutely sure Celia wasn't amongst them.

And when it was clear she wasn't, she turned away and wiped a tear from her eyes, which wasn't the result of the smoky atmosphere.

She'd felt certain Celia would have been standing amongst the survivors, wrapped in a silver blanket, and wondering like the rest of them what had just happened.

But she wasn't there, and now she had to tell her parents she had no idea if she'd perished in the flames, or if she was on her way to a different country, never to be seen again.

Neither option was going to make good hearing.

Chapter 34

Daisy seemed like the fighting spirit had been knocked out of her. She buried her face back in Aidan's shoulder. He laid his head against hers, and held her tight.

There was nothing Sarah could say to bring them any comfort, but she tried anyway. 'He might have taken her with him...'

Daisy lifted her head, glared into her eyes. 'And that helps how?'

Sarah had to look away. 'Well, not much. But at least she won't be...'

She was saved from saying the final word by the bell. The one on her phone, which seemed to jangle her nerves as it disturbed the desolate atmosphere. She almost threw it to her ear. *'What?'*

'Geez boss, you having a bad day?'

'Will? Look, I'm sorry. This isn't a good time. Things seem to have taken a turn for the worst. Maybe I'll call you later?'

'You seen it then?'

'Seen what?' she asked impatiently.

'That bonfire on the hill?'

'How do you... yes, we're here now, and my friends aren't feeling so good...'

'Did I not tell you Will.i.is is at your service, gi... boss?'

'Look Will, even your cheery smile isn't going to make much of a difference right now.'

'Don't be so sure about that. We's down by the golf course entrance as we speak. Maybe you should get your asses here.'

'We?'

'Sure. Buk and me. You coming or what... boss?'

Sarah turned to Daisy and Aidan. 'Will wants us to meet up. He's just down the road. I'll tell him no?'

Daisy glanced to Aidan. He spoke for them both. 'Tell him we'll be there, see what he wants. We've got to get out of this hell-hole anyway, and going past the golf course is on our route.'

Will heard the conversation through the phone speaker. *'See you's in ten, bosses. We's just inside the trees, opposite the entrance.'*

Sarah shook her head. Aidan was right though, they had to go back past the golf course, so it wasn't out of their way. She had no idea what Will and Buk wanted, but it wouldn't cost anything to find out.

They spotted the beat-up old Nissan, parked just off the road surrounded on three sides by palm trees. Sarah pulled up next to it.

'What the hell are they doing there?' said Daisy, her curiosity sparking her spirit up again.

'No idea,' said Sarah, climbing out of the bus. 'Let's just find out quick, and then we can go to... well, somewhere else.'

Will's grinning face hung out of the open driver's window. 'Hey guys, how's you doin?'

Daisy threw him a scowl. 'How do you think, given that we've just seen the general's house burning down?'

He nodded. 'Yeah, sure did go up good, didn't it?'

'What the hell are you doing here, anyway?' Sarah said sharply.

'Hey girl, don't be so disparaging. We got news, ok?'

'Please just tell us, quickly?' said Aidan.

Will climbed out of the minibus, followed by Buk, still in his uniform. 'Well, you see, Buk and me, we decided to carry out a little reconnaissance mission. Above and beyond the call of duty, and all that?'

'Get to the point, Will.'

'That stupid kid in the sentry box, he soon went running when Buk threatened him with a bullet. And Buk still got the gate keypad on his arm too, see?'

Buk held out his arm with a grin, so they could see for sure he still had it.

'Are you going somewhere with this, Will?' Daisy sighed.

'So we got into the house, but then we looked around a bit, decided that creep of a general didn't deserve his ill-gotten gains.'

'Can't argue there.'

'Oyite wasn't there. But them staff they didn't even know Buk wasn't a soldier anymore, so it wasn't difficult to do what we had to. That housekeeper Alice said the general had gone to Entebbe barracks to inspect the Special Forces HQ...'

'Yeah, I bet that's where he went.'

'Yeah, well, with the general out of the way, we took our opportunity, see.'

Daisy narrowed her eyes, starting to wonder if the story was going where she suspected it might be. 'Will, you didn't...'

'Sure we did. We set the fire, shouted to all the staff to get out, and then we got out too.'

Sarah threw her hands to her head in despair. 'Guys, I told you we thought there was someone else there. What the hell have you done?'

The still-grinning Will didn't seem too bothered by his boss's anguish. He walked to the rear hatch, stuck the key in the lock. 'Yeah, but you gotta understand, muzungus, things is different here in Uganda. When we take matters into our own hands, we don't hold back.'

Daisy groaned out loud, the thump of dread in her heart almost too much to bear. *'Do you realise what you did..?'* she whispered.

'Sure we do. We watched a minute or so to make sure them flames took hold, then we scarpered.'

'I can't believe this...' cried Sarah.

The grinning Will lifted the tailgate. 'I did tell you we'd see you again, remember? And we did take a few things before we left, for ourselves, you understand?'

He waved an arm to the inside of the covered luggage compartment. Daisy, Sarah and Aidan walked over and glanced inside. Will and Buk didn't seem to have taken very much before they torched the house. There was only one thing lying in the space.

It was bound and gagged, had two arms and two legs, and a white face framed by shoulder-length blonde hair.

'Celia...' Daisy choked on the single word.

'What have you done to her?' cried Sarah, ever the police officer. 'She's tied up and gagged!'

Will helped Celia to sit up, her legs dangling over the edge, a furious look in her frantic eyes. 'Well, let's say she wasn't too keen to come with us. She wanted to stay where she was and burn to death.'

Buk carefully pulled away the duck tape from her mouth, which looked a little painful even though he was trying to be gentle. 'Never knew white girls were so feisty. She fought us like a cornered gazelle. If we hadn't tied her up and stopped her screaming, we'd never have got away without anyone knowing what we'd stolen.'

None of that mattered to Daisy. She knelt down in front of her daughter, took her hand. 'Celia... we didn't think we'd ever see you again.'

Celia pierced a dull-eyed stare into her. Then she spat out the words. *'Take me home. I want to go home.'*

Aidan wiped away a tear, knelt down beside his wife. 'We are taking you home Celia, to England, just as soon as we can.'

Her misty eyes narrowed, the thin lips curled downwards. 'Why are you calling me Celia? My name is Zena. And who the hell are you anyway?'

Chapter 35

Daisy lowered her head, her body visibly sagging as Celia's words hit home. She whispered a reply. 'Celia, I'm your mother. Don't you recognise me?'

'I don't have a mother. Take me home. I want to go home.'

Aidan put a hand around his wife's dejected shoulders. 'We have to give her time, dear. It's been three years, and she's probably been...'

The words faded away, Aidan reluctant to say the rest of the sentence. As Daisy got to her feet and staggered a few steps away from the minibus, Sarah finished it for him. 'Drugged up to the eyeballs, Daisy. Sorry, but it has to be said.'

Daisy looked round, her eyes full of tears. 'My own daughter didn't recognise me, Sarah.'

'I know. But she will. And getting her out of this environment will help.'

Suddenly they caught movement out of the corner of their eyes. Celia was on the move, bolting for what she believed was her life. Buk was quickest to react, helped by the fact Celia's legs didn't seem to want to work so well. He grabbed her, dragged her back to the minibus.

'Get your filthy hands off me... I want to go home.'

Will put his face right in front of hers. 'You ain't got a home anymore, girl. Not in Uganda anyways.'

'You're lying to me. Emmanuel will kill you for this.'

'I very much doubt that, hun.'

Aidan ran up to his daughter, tried to wrap his arms around her. She pushed him away, tears streaming down her face. 'Leave me alone, all of you. Just get lost, I'll walk home.'

'Got a boat?' Will asked her.

'Ok, this isn't helping.' Sarah eased Aidan and Will away. 'Look, one or two people over at the golf course are watching us a little curiously. We need to get out of here, now.'

'What, with this one spitting fire?' said Will.

'I... Daisy, what do we do?'

She threw desolate hands in the air. 'How should I know? I didn't really expect our reunion to be like this.'

Aidan pulled her close. 'Dear, she's been under the influence of someone else for three years. God only knows what he's pumped into her, but her memories before then have been... suppressed. She doesn't know any different right now. But you've got to accept this might take a little time.'

'Why do you always have to be so bloody sensible, Dip?' she glared an accusation at him.

He let out a little chuckle. 'Well, one of us has to be. But Sarah's right, we've got to get away from those prying eyes.'

'How, dear? Are you suggesting we kidnap our own daughter?'

Sarah threw a hand into the air. 'Might be the only way, Daisy.'

'You have got to be kidding me.'

Will waved the roll of duck tape in the air. 'Got plenty of tape!'

'Seriously?'

'I want to go home...'

Daisy glanced to her still-struggling daughter, then at Will and Buk, finally at Sarah, and then sank her head into

182

Aidan's shoulder without a word. He spoke for them both. 'Do it, guys.'

As she watched the cornered gazelle called Celia trussed up once more, and a ring of duck tape wrapped around her mouth again, Daisy felt her heart shattering into a million pieces. She put a hand on Celia's face, just before the tailgate was dropped again.

'I know you won't believe it dear, but this is for your own good. It's hurting me more than it's hurting you, trust me.'

A spate of expletives were thrown back at her, but luckily the tape meant they came out as mumbled, indiscernible grunts.

Will closed the tailgate, much to Daisy's desolation, and jumped back in the driving seat. 'Where to, boss?'

Sarah answered. 'The British embassy, to pick up Anton. You know where it is?' He nodded. 'We'll follow you in the Volkswagen.'

Daisy and Aidan slipped back into the bus, and the two vehicles drove away. Daisy wrapped a trembling hand around Aidan's. 'So glad we've got two cars, dear. I don't think I could stomach being in the same vehicle as our daughter right now.'

Just before they reached the centre of Kampala, Daisy's phone rang. Anton's slightly-jittery voice said the words that confirmed his nervousness.

'Geez, I wasn't sure you'd even be able to reply, Petal.'

'You know me, Anton. Still alive and kicking.'

'Hell girl, I'm standing in the car park looking at a pall of smoke drifting from Kololo way.'

'Yes, it's the general's house. Not that there will be much left of it by now.'

The voice hesitated. *'What have you done, Daisy?'*

183

'It wasn't us, Anton. Someone else didn't seem to care much for him either.'

'Aw hell... what about Celia?'

'We've got her. Not that she wanted to come with us.'

The words were sighed out. *'Thank god for that. The general?'*

'Not there. He told the housekeeper he was going to Entebbe barracks first thing this morning. Something about inspecting the troops, if you believe that.'

'Entebbe? Hell, I hope he didn't, given what's just happened.'

'What's at Entebbe? And what do you mean, what's just happened?'

'Entebbe is the HQ of the Special Forces Command. Think back to the German Secret Service. They're just as bad. And I've convinced the ambassador Oyite is the bad guy. While I was there he was on the phone to the Ugandan authorities, so things are going to kick off... probably as we speak.'

'Even that might be too late, Anton. I think the general already got wind of it, and he's on the run. He likely played a round of golf with the Inspector General.'

'Let's hope he's gone. But if he is still around, it ain't safe for you guys right now. Retaliation is pretty big around here. You need to lay low until we can get you out.'

'We're going to need your help, Anton. For one thing, Celia hasn't got a passport, so we can't just jump on an Emirates flight home.'

'Well aware of that. Where are you now?'

'Two minutes away from you. We need an exit strategy, Anton.'

He hesitated, like he was thinking hard. *'Ok, first we need to get you off the mainland. Somewhere no one knows where you are. I'll see what I can sort, but just for now I'll take you to my island. We can hang out there, until we can get you out of Africa.'*

Daisy clicked off the call. They were just about to drive into the embassy car park, and she could see Anton standing waiting just a little way from the main building.

'Looks like we're going to end our trip to Africa on an island paradise,' she said to the others, not at all convinced *paradise* was the right word.

Chapter 36

Anton's eyes flicked around the inside of the bus. 'I thought you said you'd rescued Celia? I can't see her.'

'She's in the Nissan,' said Daisy, pointing to the minibus standing a few yards away. Anton looked over. 'I still can't see her.'

'She's in the back,' called Will from the driver's seat.

'The... the back?'

'Ain't no time to explain now. Let's just say she ain't being cooperative, yeah?'

Anton looked at Daisy with raised eyebrows. *'What?'*

Sarah saved Daisy the embarrassment. 'Anton, just get in. It's too public here.' She shouted over to Will. 'Let's go somewhere more private... out on the Entebbe road, where we can... switch the cargo, ok?'

He nodded, floored the throttle. Sarah followed him out of the car park, and Anton narrowed his eyes at Daisy and Aidan. 'Would somebody tell me what's going on?'

'Well, we didn't put any bullet-holes in the hire car, my friend.'

He shook his head, but then Aidan brought him up to speed, which resulted in more head-shakes.

'Your head will fall off in a minute, Anton,' Daisy found a smile.

'Geez girl, when I said the shit would hit the fan, I didn't expect you to be the one throwing it.'

'Are you implying we've made some kind of impression on Uganda, Anton?'

As Sarah drove, Anton called the American ambassador In Nairobi. He explained the situation as quickly as he could, which was received by a few groans and sharp intakes of breath, from both ends of the phone. It didn't sound like the ambassador was too pleased by some of the things he was told, but he did tell Anton the British ambassador had already been in touch with him, and made him aware of the potential international incident they'd all been responsible for creating.

But he was all too aware the catalyst of the trouble had to be removed from the firing line as soon as possible. And just as aware it had to be done without creating a *double* international incident.

Anton killed the call, blew out his cheeks. 'Geez, I don't often make phone calls as stressful as that.'

Daisy looked concerned. 'Are you in diplomatic trouble now?'

'Nothing I can't handle. Unlike you, I really do have diplomatic immunity! The ambassador I can handle.'

'I'm so sorry we seem to have caused an international incident.'

'Yeah well... the ambassador agrees we've got to remove you before... anything else happens. I told him I'm taking you to the island, so he's trying to make plans to get you away from there, which will almost certainly involve the Kenyan Air Force. But it can't be until tonight, under the cover of darkness. Geez, it's like the *Raid on Entebbe* all over again.'

'I really didn't want to be so much trouble, Anton.'

He squeezed her hand. 'Hey, don't worry about it. It's the most action I've had in years!'

The Nissan up ahead pulled over in a quiet part of the highway screened by a copse of trees. Sarah came to a stop just behind the minibus. Will had chosen the right spot, where prying eyes on the busy road wouldn't see what they didn't want anyone to see.

The streets and houses of Kampala were behind them; ahead was the beautiful countryside stretching southwards to Entebbe. Right there all seemed peaceful and safe, but as Daisy climbed out of the car, the all-too-familiar thump of dread churned her stomach inside out again.

She knew just as well as Anton that given what they were responsible for starting, safety was hardly guaranteed until they were away from Africa. But there was another reason for the stomach churning. Once more she was about to come face-to-face with a daughter who didn't recognise her, and who she'd allowed to be trussed up like an oven-ready turkey.

Will lifted the tailgate, and Daisy's gut wrapped itself into an impossible knot. Celia was helped out of the trunk, her green eyes still flaming anger. Anton tried to smile to her. 'Good to finally meet you, Celia. Maybe not in the best of circumstances, that's for sure. If we take away the tape, will you promise not to scream like a banshee?'

Celia nodded, her eyes still flicking manically around the people who had kidnapped her. Anton pulled off the duck tape, as gently as he could. 'Thank you, Celia,' he said softly.

'My name is Zena. Why do you keep calling me Celia?' she spat out, and then glared at Daisy. 'And I want to know who you are. You look familiar. Are you the cook or something?'

Daisy turned away, and then felt Aidan's arms around her. 'Hold it together, dear. That's a good sign... she said you look familiar.'

'Yeah, she thinks I'm the cook, Dip.'

Anton was untying the ropes around Celia's wrists and ankles. 'I'm going to get rid of these... Zena. We need you to

188

come with us, but no one wants to harm you. No kicking off, ok?'

'I don't have much of a choice, do I?' she growled.

'No, you don't. So just accept this is for the best.' He led her to the Volkswagen's rear seat, made sure she sat in it. 'Aidan, maybe you should sit beside her, do what you can to keep her calm?'

He nodded, climbed into the bus. Anton walked over to Will and Buk, shook their hands. 'It seems we owe you both a big thank you. But now you've put your own safety at risk.'

Will smiled, a little uncertainly. 'Aw man, we's survivors. We'll go to ground for a while, it'll be ok.'

Anton handed him his business card. 'Fair enough, but just in case, if shit happens you call me. The British ambassador here is a friend, so if needs be we'll do what we can to make sure you're safe.'

'Gee, thanks, man.'

Sarah walked over to him, gave him a long hug. 'Hey deputy, thank you so much for your service, above and beyond the call of duty.' She kissed him on the cheek. 'And for being there, beside me.'

He looked totally embarrassed, but then glanced up and grinned ruefully. 'And we didn't get our night on the town after all.'

She nodded. 'Yeah, I know. If things were different, just know I'd be proud to let you show me the sights, Will.'

'Aw geez, you's making me go red now.'

'You're Ugandan, Will. You don't go red.'

'Nah, but I am inside.'

'I'll take that as a compliment.'

'Sure. Hey, can I have the RPKS as a keepsake?'

'In your dreams.'

189

She hugged him again, and then did the same for Buk, and the two of them climbed back into the Nissan and drove away in a cloud of dust. Sarah put her arm around Daisy. 'Come on you, we've got to find that tropical island paradise.'

Fortunately, the Volkswagen had two sets of rear seats. Daisy and Sarah dropped into the second set, and Anton jumped in behind the wheel. 'Ok folks, settle in. Less than an hour, and we should be headed across the water to my home.'

Daisy glanced behind her, tried to smile at her scowling daughter, who tried to pretend she hadn't noticed. Aidan reached out, took her hand, nodded encouragingly but didn't say a word. Daisy gave him a smile she really wasn't feeling, and then turned back to face forwards. It was better than looking back at the daughter who was breaking her heart.

Aidan looked Celia over, trying not to let her see he was. Her eyes were firmly fixed through the window, so it wasn't too difficult to watch her. She was still dressed in a pair of shorts and top that looked like nightwear, the short-sleeved T-shirt revealing the pale skin of her arms. He groaned his dismay silently to himself. Their daughter had never carried any excess weight, but now she looked slimmer than ever.

Her left arm carried the signs of what she'd been through for the last three years. Just before the elbow were several red pinpricks, clearly the result of the general or his loyal staff shooting her full of something that made her a willing captive, and helped the real memories of who she was fade away.

Bringing her back to the reality she deserved was for sure not going to happen overnight.

190

They drove along the same road through Entebbe they'd headed the opposite way along just a week before. Then, as they left the town, and just before the road that branched off to the airport, Anton threw a left.

They passed a couple of smart-looking beach hotel resorts, and then in front of them was a single-storey bar that seemed like it was made of logs, standing on the shore of the lake. It was just gone lunchtime, and the sandy forecourt was packed with people sitting at wooden tables enjoying drinks and a little food. Anton drove over to the far corner of the parking area, but it still wasn't that far from the punters enjoying the sunshine.

'Ok folks, it's just a short walk from here to the quay, but this is as far as we can go with wheels.' He nodded to an open Landrover parked a few cars away. 'And it's not unusual, but the army are here too. Favourite drinking establishment for the Special Forces stationed just up the road. So be careful.'

They climbed out of the bus, grabbed their luggage, and the sports bag. Anton nodded to a set of padlocked double gates at the rear of the car park. 'That's the way,' he said quietly. Then he nodded in the direction of one of the tables, where five Ugandan men in SF uniforms were laughing together as they enjoyed a few bottles of beer.

'We could do without them sitting there.'

Daisy nodded her agreement, but as they walked nonchalantly towards the gates, Celia spotted the men too. Aidan had his arm in hers, in what he'd thought was a firm hold that didn't look suspicious. It wasn't firm enough.

She wriggled free, and before anyone realised what was happening, she was heading for the five army men.

'Help... these people have kidnapped me!'

191

Chapter 37

Anton was quickest to react. He raced after Celia, wrapped restraining arms around her waist just before she reached the army men. 'Sorry, guys. She's… um… not very well. A little stupid, if you get me.'

'I'm not stupid. I want to go ho…'

He slapped a hand across her mouth, just as Sarah ran up, flashed her badge. 'Officer Lowry, police. Sorry about this, chaps. Nothing to worry about, but this is an international civilian matter, so… um… don't concern yourselves.'

They manhandled Celia back to her parents. Daisy looked like her world had just caved in. Anton glared at Celia. *'Just chill, ok?* You're not going to get away, so give it up.'

'You called me stupid. That's a real insult in this part of the world.'

He fumbled with the lock on the gates. 'You are stupid, girl, if you think we don't have your best interests at heart.'

Aidan took over restraining duties as Anton threw open the gates. As they walked through onto a dirt track leading to the shore, Daisy glanced back. 'One of those army guys has just whipped his communicator out,' she said flatly.

Anton pulled a frustrated expression. 'That's as maybe, but we're almost away. Shift your butts, folks.'

They half-ran, half-walked onto the wooden quay. A few boats were tied up. 'Is that yours?' said Sarah, pointing at a big launch with an open cabin.

'Nah, it's that one.'

'Seriously? That's a dinghy with an outboard!'

192

'Now you're insulting it. And it's got two outboards. But I can go spend a few hours finding you a luxury cruiser if you like?'

'Don't bother,' Sarah grinned. 'You sure we'll all fit in?'

Anton grinned back. 'It might be okay when we get up on the plane, but before that...'

'Now *you're* starting to wind me up.'

They all scrambled aboard, Celia still kicking and screaming in protest. Anton unlocked the engine controls, and the two massive outboards growled their way to life. He stood in front of the steering console poking from the centre of the open boat, and Sarah and Daisy untied the mooring ropes.

Then, just as she was coiling up the rope, Daisy glanced back to the shore. As the boat moved slowly away from the quay, she saw something she really didn't want to see.

'You have got to be kidding me...'

A vehicle had pulled up to the gates. A very smart vehicle. It looked like a black Bentley, with a Ugandan flag attached to a pole on its front bumper. And a very smartly-dressed man had opened the rear door, and was watching them disappear.

This time he wasn't wearing a black gown with gold lapels. This time he had all of his medals and commendations glinting in the light of the afternoon sun. And even from two hundred yards away, the expression on his face was enough to fill the hearts of anyone who saw it with terror.

Anton glanced back as he thrust the twin throttles to full. 'What... oh, shit.'

193

Sarah looked at him with real fear in her eyes. 'Looks like our favourite general told his housekeeper the truth after all. He *was* inspecting the troops in Entebbe.'

Daisy narrowed her eyes. 'Of all the barracks in all the world, he had to be in ours.'

The bow of the boat rose into the air as Anton cleared the quayside. 'Hang onto your hats, folks. This is gonna be a full-speed roller coaster of a ride.'

Two miles away across the glinting water of the lake, which looked just like an ocean and had waves to prove it, they could see three islands, arranged in a line. Sitting a mile or two from each other, the biggest of them, on the right, looked to be populated, a shanty town built up around the shore. The middle one was smaller, hilly, and seemed to consist of nothing but trees.

The one on the left, which Anton was heading for, was also really small, and also seemed to consist of nothing but trees. 'That's ours...' he called out, pointing at it.

'I can't see your house,' Sarah shouted back over the noise of the outboards.

'It's on the far side, next to a tiny beach.'

Daisy, in the rear of the boat, was keeping an eye out behind them. The general's car had left, and she breathed a slight sigh of relief. Despite the fact much of it bordered one of the biggest lakes in the world, Uganda was in fact landlocked. It didn't possess a navy. It was starting to look like they'd got away clean.

That didn't last long.

From behind a peninsular a mile away, a fast boat had appeared. To begin with Daisy tried to tell herself it was simply rich Ugandans out for a joyride. It wasn't much bigger than the rather-crowded one they were on, and open

194

like their own. But as it grew closer, she had to bat away those thoughts rather quickly.

She could make out six men sitting in the little boat heading rapidly on an intercept course. And six automatic rifles, the front two of which seemed to be pointing right at them.

'*Guys...*' she cried.

Anton looked round in horror. It might have been Daisy's cry, but it was more likely the bullet that seared into the waves twenty feet away. He let out a few expletives, and then glanced meaningfully to Daisy. As a hail of bullets smacked into the water one after the other, and Anton began to steer evasive manoeuvres, she fumbled in the sports bag.

'Dear, you can't...' gasped Aidan.

'*I want to go home,*' screamed Celia.

'I'm not going to shoot anyone, Dip. Despite the fact they're trying to kill us. I'm just going to disable them.'

'I don't believe this,' cried Sarah. 'We're in the middle of a hail of bullets, on the sea, in an *inflatable boat*?'

'Semi-inflatable,' corrected Anton.

'Oh well, that's all right then. Only half of it is filled with air.'

'You complaining again?'

Sarah didn't get chance to reply. The clatter of the RPKS sounded louder than the growl of the engines as Daisy let off a five-second burst.'

'Anton, keep it steady for a second.'

'Dear, please don't shoot anyone.'

'Dip, please shut up. I'm trying to sink their boat.'

'Oh, please forgive me.'

Another five-second burst, and Daisy grinned at Aidan. 'Sorry dear, but needs must.'

He cast his eyes back to the chasing boat. Daisy's streak of bullets had ripped away the entire port side of the boat just beneath the waterline, and the six men and their rifles were getting rather wet. One of the still-standing lifted his rifle to retaliate, but then the boat disappeared beneath him, and he was suddenly far too preoccupied trying to keep from drowning.

'I'm sure they'll be rescued,' said Daisy, even though she was not at all sure.

A minute later they were out of sight of the men without a boat, as Anton cruised a little more slowly a couple of hundred yards off the right-hand shore of the island. Still there wasn't anything to see other than trees, but then as they rounded the point on the southern tip of the island, a beautiful beach broke the greenery with its golden sand.

Anton brought the boat alongside a tiny landing stage, and Sarah tied it to the weathered round posts that resembled saw-off palm-tree trunks.

'*I want to go home,*' mumbled a slightly more subdued Celia.

'You are home,' Anton grinned. 'My home!'

Chapter 38

Sarah shielded her eyes from the afternoon sun with her hand, peered across the beach to the house nestled just inside the tree line.

'I thought you said it was a house?'

'It is a house.'

'It's a *shack*!'

'Ok, it's a tropical beach house. But a very nice shack all the same.'

Celia stamped her feet like a spoilt child, as much as she could on the soft sand. 'I want to go home.'

Anton grinned. 'Sure, off you go then.'

She stomped away in the direction of the trees.

'Mind the snakes, by the way.'

She stopped stomping, turned and glared at him. 'Snakes?'

'Yeah, this island is full of them. Got plenty of antidote in the house, but if you're out there on your own...'

'Ok,' she growled. 'Maybe I'll stay here. *For now*.'

Aidan took her hand, led her gently towards the house. She narrowed her eyes at him. 'I've seen you somewhere before. Are you the gardener?'

He nodded his head slowly. 'Yeah, Zena. I'm the gardener.'

Anton glanced to Daisy, saw the desolate look in her eyes. 'She'll be okay, kid. Once you get her away from here, it'll all come back to her.'

She slipped an arm around him as they headed for the house. 'Right now I wish I was a kid again. Might have avoided all the heartache of being a mother.'

Anton was right, it was a very nice shack. Just one bedroom, the biggest part of it was open plan. Made entirely from felled trees, it almost felt like a holiday cabin on the shores of Lake Michigan. A smart kitchen area that definitely didn't come from the island took up one corner of the big room. The rest of the space was filled with a couple of lounging sofas, and a wide-screen TV, sitting on the wall above an iron fire grate set in a stone-lined fireplace.

'A fireplace, in Uganda?' said Aidan. 'Now I know why you dress like a hillbilly!'

Anton laughed. 'Don't believe everything you read on the internet. Right here it gets pretty cold some nights, and my hillbilly upbringing seems to like real flames and smoke curling up from a chimney.'

'What's in there?' said Daisy, pointing to a door next to the fireplace.

'Thought you might ask that. Come on, I'll show you.' He opened the door, beckoned her inside. She let out a whistle. 'I know you like mementos, Anton, but this..?'

The small room, built onto the outside wall as a lean-to, was full of things that would never pass through a custom's checkpoint. Two of the walls were lined with brackets holding the biggest collection of hand weapons she'd seen outside a military museum. In a glass-fronted case sitting against the third wall, a few different kinds of mementos were on display.

'Grenades? Detonators?'

He grinned. 'Most of this stuff most likely doesn't even work anymore. Apart from the RPKS I brought you.'

She nodded ruefully. 'Ok, I'll give you that. Kind of glad you kept memories. But most of this stuff is almost as old as I am.'

He laughed. 'Yeah, but just as R.E.D., I guess. I started... collecting right from my first year in the CIA. Now I'm not active anymore... well, I guess I'm finding it hard to let go.'

'I'm glad we could oblige, give you something to do to keep you on the ball.'

'Geez, you sure did that.'

The phone in his pocket buzzed. He answered. 'Hey, Frank. Was just about to call you. We're here now. Had a little excitement on the way over. Seems General Oyite is still on the loose.'

The ambassador sucked in a deep breath. *'Everyone ok?'*

'Sure. We had to sink the enemy patrol boat though.'

'This is not good, Anton. Maybe my news is coming just in time. We've arranged for a Kenyan helicopter to pick you up, fly you to Laikipia Air Base in Nanyuki, which as you know is also the other base for the BATUK barracks. There's a British supply aircraft just landed there, so our British friends can sneak a lift home when it flies back to Essex tomorrow.'

'Frank, I can't thank you enough. But there's nowhere for a helicopter to land here. This strip of beach is way too soft and narrow.'

'There's no other way to get them out of Uganda quickly. And quite frankly, the sooner they're gone the sooner we can start patching up relations. They'll just have to be winched up in a cradle.'

'What, again?' said Daisy, screwing up her face.

'That's ok, Frank. How long?'

'Not until dark. Nine this evening, so you'll have to kick your heels for six hours.'

'Thanks again, Frank. I owe you one.'

You owe me about two hundred. But we'll talk about that when you're next in the office. Good luck.'

Anton clicked off the call, shook his head. 'Sure got a bit of explaining to do,' he said ruefully.

Daisy put a hand on his arm. 'None of this would have been possible without you, Anton. Let's just hope you don't lose your job over it.'

'Nah. But if I do, it ain't that big a deal. Was thinking of retiring in a couple of years anyways. Kinda like being here in this *shack* with the right company.'

'You know what, my friend? I kind of envy you.'

Anton fired up the generator, and they boiled about five kettles of water to fill pasta-pots from his emergency stash. He didn't keep much fresh food in the house, shopping before he and Enid spent each weekend there, cruising the supplies over in the boat with them.

And he'd sure as hell not had time to food shop on this occasion.

But there was always a stash of dried snacks in stock, just in case people got hungry. There weren't many pasta pots left when they'd all had their fill, and not much bottled water either.

The sun was disappearing behind the hill in the centre of the island, and there was just three hours to go until the cavalry arrived, when Daisy suddenly noticed Celia was missing.

'Where's our daughter, dear?'

He looked around the room, even though he already knew she wasn't there. 'Gone to the loo?' he offered.

'Don't think so,' said Sarah. 'I saw her come out of the bathroom just a few minutes ago.'

Daisy got to her weary feet. 'I'll go see where she is. Maybe she's sitting outside.'

She wasn't sitting outside. The door to Anton's memorabilia room burst open, and a frantic-eyed Celia stood there, nervously waving an automatic rifle at them.

'Get that stupid boat of yours fired up, Anton. I'm going home, and you're taking me… now!'

Chapter 39

Anton tried to smile reassuringly. 'Celia, put the gun down. This is pointless. We're your friends.'

'I'm not Celia. My name is Zena. How many more times?'

Her dull eyes were darting manically from side to side, the barrel of the gun flicking scarily from one shocked kidnapper to the other. She was one step from losing it completely.

'Ok... Zena, put the gun down,' said Aidan softly.

'Leave me alone...'

Shaking hands gripped the rifle a little tighter, and a finger curled around the trigger. Then she lifted the weapon to the coconut-wood ceiling and pressed the trigger, intending to fire a few rounds to make a relevant point.

The firing chamber let out a sigh of a hiss, but the gun didn't fire.

Everyone in the room knew it wouldn't. Celia's drug-confused mind hadn't even realised she'd not loaded a magazine. There were no bullets to fire.

Her crazed eyes looked up to the ceiling like she couldn't believe what hadn't happened. Then the gun clattered to the wooden floor. Two seconds later she followed it, crumpling to her knees and crying out in despair.

Sarah was the first to reach her, dropping to her knees beside the distraught girl. 'Hey Celia... it's ok. We will get you home.' She reached out an arm to pull her close, but Celia thrust it away, her eyes flaming fire through the tears.

'Who the hell are you anyway? It's like looking in a mirror looking at you.'

Sarah had to smile. 'I'm your friend. Maybe your clone, if you like?'

'Get lost, bitch.'

Daisy snapped. The adrenaline had flowed like white-water in the last few days, and coupled with the still-present fear they weren't yet safe, and the sight of her daughter pointing a lethal weapon at her mother... suddenly it all became too much. She stomped over to Celia, and stood over her with a look of thunder piercing through the rain of tears.

Her voice was cracked with emotion as she thundered out the words. 'You listen to me girl, and you listen good. Have you any idea what we've been through to rescue you, you ungrateful cow? Start acting like an appreciative adult instead of a teenage brat, ok?'

No one moved. The world went to freeze-frame as everyone stared open mouthed at Daisy, unable to quite believe what they'd just heard.

Everyone except Celia.

As the tears of defeat rolled down her cheeks, she still managed to spit out defiant words.

'Geez... get off my back, ok? You sound like my mother...'

Still no one moved. Suddenly Celia stopped sobbing, and slowly lifted her eyes to Daisy, a hundred jumbled questions tumbling through the gloss of silent tears.

'Mum..?'

Daisy dropped to her knees, the tears she'd almost kept under control for the last few days finally letting go. She pulled her daughter into her, and as they held each other like they would never let go, the desolation, heartbreak and hopelessness of three years of life poured out in an unstoppable torrent.

'Mum... I don't know who I am any more...'

203

Daisy managed to whisper through the pain and the joy. 'You will, Celia Henderson. We'll make sure you know who you are again, I promise.'

Aidan dropped down beside them, made it an emotional group hug. Sarah wiped away a tear of her own, turned to Anton. 'She was shaking like a leaf in a hurricane, even before the reunion.'

He shook his head, glanced at his watch. 'She's going cold turkey. Still three hours until the chopper. I ain't got nothing here to help, but they will have at Laikipia. She's not going to be feeling so good by the time they get there though, I gotta say.'

Daisy and Anton sat side by side on the edge of the beach, the line of palm trees right behind them, fifty yards away from the house. Darkness was just pulling its blanket over the island, and they'd all decided it might be best to keep an eye on the water, in case Oyite sent any more boats full of soldiers to exterminate them.

Aidan and Sarah were inside with Celia, keeping her company, and gently bringing her up to speed with the last three years. Not that she was totally aware of what was going on around her. Anton had found some aspirin, and she was stretched out on one of the sofas, spaced out but feeling calmer.

That wasn't likely to last too long. It was still two hours until their airlift arrived, and no one was sure how chilled out she might not be by then.

Daisy and Anton had volunteered for water-watch duties, and both of them had taken up position just inside the tree line, out of sight of anyone arriving by boat. Both had weapons in their hands.

'This remind you of anything?' Anton grinned.

204

'Course it does. Hiding on an African beach, watching out for incoming enemy boats. How could it not?'

He let out a little chuckle. 'You could say we've come full circle, Petal.'

She smiled warmly to him. 'Don't expect me to take my top off for you this time, Anton.'

'That was something I ain't gonna forget though. Kinda precious, you might say.'

Daisy nodded, deep in recall. 'It was... special. The kind of special you don't ever not remember.'

'Tell me about it. But special or not, we weren't right for each other, long term. Then we were both lucky enough to find the ones who were.'

'I never thought I would though, Anton. Not in my line of work.'

'Me either. But we did. And now here we sit, back to twelve on our clock, reminiscing about click number one.'

'Hey, we've not passed midnight yet, dear boy. Plenty of clicks to go yet.'

'Glad we spent another one together though, girl.'

She rested her head on his shoulder. 'Me too,' she said quietly. 'Even leaving aside the fact you had to save my life... again.'

'It's a dirty job, but someone's got to do it.'

'That's what Aidan and Sarah say. Am I that bad?'

'Well...'

She lifted her head, smiled to him. 'I shall take that as a compliment.'

'That's your choice, girl.'

'Ok, just shut up now.'

The conversation died. As the last of the light faded to blackness, and a million stars began to puncture the night sky, it felt just like the deserted beach near Mombasa. But

Daisy was thinking of something much more recent than that.

'I lost it with Celia, Anton.'

'From what I saw, it got good results.'

'But as I told you three years ago, it was because I couldn't cope any more that Celia got taken in the first place.'

'Any loving mother would have a hard time watching her daughter throw her life away.'

'That's not the point. I got to the edge then, and again a couple of hours ago. I just couldn't take any more. I broke. And I know making Celia better is going to have moments that will be just as hard to cope with. What happens if I reach the edge again, Anton?'

He wrapped a hand around hers. 'You ever heard of breaking in a stallion?'

'This is my daughter. Not a wild horse.'

'Maybe. But a couple of hours ago she was a wild horse. Back where I come from, they used to break horses all the time. That cowboy... or cowgirl, would work at that wild horse, sometimes for days. But when that goddamn horse broke, it stayed broke, and grew to enjoy its new life.'

'What are you saying?'

'Maybe you didn't intend to, but you were the cowgirl who broke that horse called Celia. Ok, that's a harsh way of putting it, but that's what happened. Now she's back in the family, and the worst is over. You ain't gonna reach your edge, Petal. These last few days have thrown a container-load of shit at you. In a strange land too, for god's sake. Once you all get back to familiar territory, the rest is gonna be a breeze... well, you know what I mean.

'Thank you, Anton. I do know what you mean. I don't think it will be a breeze... but you still said the right things to keep me on the straight and narrow.'

'Any time, Petal.'

The need for any more words died away. Silently they sat, both of them gazing out over an empty lake, watching the gentle waves breaking over the narrow strip of beach. A half- moon rose into the sky, pooling a gentle light across the water, and making it easier to see anything that wasn't too welcome.

Daisy glanced at her watch. One hour to go. She was just about to suggest to Anton she popped back to the house to see how Celia was, when they both heard something.

Something they really didn't expect to hear.

Chapter 40

A muffled thud broke the silence, coming from a distance away. Daisy looked at Anton. 'What was that?'

He shook his head. 'That's all we need. The Special Forces Command has a small artillery barracks on the peninsula, two miles away. Once a month, on a weekday, they practice by firing shells at the island they acquired for target practice. That one...'

He pointed across the water to a tiny dark shape, jutting out of the water just over a mile away.

Daisy raised her eyebrows. 'Let's hope they don't get wildly inaccurate, drop one here instead.'

He laughed. 'Don't worry, they're pretty well trained. We're safe.'

'They're firing from a distance. What artillery are they using?'

'There's a couple of old Howitzers based there.'

'Seriously? Where the hell did they get M3's from?'

'Russia, I think.'

'You've got to be kidding me. Now we really have gone full circle.'

He grinned. 'It never lasts very long. Won't stop the chopper getting here... it'll be over in half an hour.'

Then, just as he said that, a new noise filled the air. Daisy looked at him wide-eyed. 'That sounds awfully like a shell about to land.'

'*Geez...*'

There wasn't time to say anymore. The plummeting shell hit the ground and exploded, in the trees two hundred yards behind them.

They scrambled to their feet. 'I though you said they were well-trained?'

'They are. Oh hell...'

'What?'

'I've just remembered who the general-in-charge of the Special Forces is.'

'Are you winding me up again?'

'Wish I was.'

Anton sprinted for the house, Daisy right behind him. As they made the door, another shell struck the ground, a little closer this time.

Aidan threw them a look with fear written all over it. 'What the hell was that?'

Anton ran to the sofa, helped a semi-conscious Celia to her feet. 'Everybody out, quick. This house will be like an ammunition dump if a shell hits it!'

Daisy and Aidan slipped supportive arms around Celia, headed for the door as quickly as they could. 'Did I say thank you for saving my life, collector of memorabilia?' she glared at Anton.

'How was I supposed to know this was going to happen?' he called back, as he grabbed the satellite phone.

'Is someone trying to kill me?' mumbled Celia, half awake.

'Yeah. That thug you know so well, Emmanuel,' said Daisy.

They staggered out of the shack, and almost fell onto the soft sand of the strip of beach which served as its front garden. Anton virtually dragged them another hundred yards. A shell exploded in the trees behind them.

'That was closer,' gasped Aidan.

The next shell wasn't closer. It was spot on.

As they threw themselves to the sand and covered their heads, the shack exploded into a million pieces.

Daisy batted away a couple of small pieces of branch and palm leaf. She looked around to the others as they sat up slowly. 'Everyone ok?'

They all nodded, in a somewhat dazed way. Aidan had a cut on his head, but it wasn't anything life-threatening. They'd managed to get out of the shack with a minute to spare.

Anton struggled to his feet, looked at the devastation. *'Aw, hell.'*

Daisy stood up beside him. 'I'm so sorry, Anton. It's all my fault.'

He put a hand on her shoulder. 'Nah... it's all part of making things right, Daisy. The authorities can foot the bill for building a new one, once Oyite is brought to justice.'

She shook her head. 'And when is that going to be, Anton? Seems to me he's still very much in control right now.'

He lifted his arms from his sides. 'I don't know.'

Another shell thumped into the ground, a little further away this time. Anton glanced over to the landing stage. 'The stage is still standing. I can just see the peninsula from there. At least we'll know how many shells they're firing at us!'

He ran across the sand. Daisy ran too, just behind him, and then along the narrow gangway to the slightly-wider landing stage with the boat moored to it. She looked in amazement at the semi-inflatable.

'All that debris and the boat full of air is still in one piece?'

'Told you it was sturdy.'

She shook her head, followed Anton's gaze back to the mainland. He pointed out the peninsula, seconds before he didn't need to, as the flash of a Howitzer firing its shell momentarily lit up the coastline two miles across the water.

'Here comes another one.'

They waited for it to hit home. It smacked into the ground on the other side of the island.

'Bad shot,' said Anton.

'I'll pretend you didn't say that.'

'You know what I mean.'

They watched as two more flashes lit up the peninsula, waited as the shells crashed into the island. One was way off the mark, one not so far from being a danger to life.

'We don't need one any closer than that,' said Daisy nervously.

Then, a louder sound filled the air. As they watched for the guns to fire again, a different kind of thud resonated across the mainland two miles away. A huge ball of flames climbed into the air, just behind where the guns were positioned.

Daisy whispered to Anton. 'What was that?'

He looked as confused as she did. 'No idea. Something's gone up, big time.'

They watched for another three minutes. Whatever it was that exploded was sending balls of flame into the night sky, and a pall of black smoke began to drift across the water.

Anton shook his head. 'Whatever it was, it seems to have helped matters.'

The firing had stopped. It seemed like the Special Forces Command had more urgent matters to attend to.

Chapter 41

Anton's phone crackled into life.

'We're three miles out, Mr. Kowalski. Please get everyone ready.'

'Cheers, guys. We're already outside, waiting.'

He didn't tell the chopper crew they didn't have much choice, the only inside space on the island now a pile of debris surrounding them. 'Almost time to say goodbye, folks.'

'Will you be alright, my friend?'

He pulled Daisy into a hug. 'Sure, Petal. The boat is still in one piece, and all seems to be calm now. I'll head to Masaka, spend a few days with my better half and her sister, while I find out what's gone down and wait for my punishment!'

'I feel so bad, Anton. We seem to have caused a lot of devastation, one way or another.'

'You just worry about putting your family back together. Wouldn't have missed it for the world... and if I'm not mistaken we righted a few wrongs. It's a win, whichever way I look at it.'

'I think you're putting a brave face on it, my friend. Thank you.'

She held him tight for a moment. The sound of helicopter blades were thumping their beat into the night air, and from the direction of the Kenyan shore, two bright lights were heading towards them.

Anton shook Aidan's hand, gave him a man-hug. Then he embraced Sarah, and did the same to Celia. She looked half-asleep, and her body was starting to shake again. 'You gonna promise me you'll let those do-or-die parents of yours show you what real love is now, kid?'

She nodded feebly. 'I promise. Thanks, Anton.'

Then all was light and sound. The chopper was hovering twenty feet above the landing stage. It wasn't safe to get any closer. A rope ladder dropped from the open door, followed by a rescue cradle, a Kenyan sergeant winching it down, together with a female member of the crew.

She made the landing stage just as Anton shepherded his guests onto it. Aidan began to climb the rope ladder, followed by Sarah. Daisy and the army girl helped Celia into the cradle, and she watched as it was winched into the belly of the helicopter.

Through the noise of the rotors she shouted to Anton. *'I don't know how to thank you. Just saying that doesn't seem enough.'*

He laughed. *'Maybe if we get an invite to Norfolk soon, it might make me feel a bit better!'*

'You can consider that carved in stone, Anton.'

'I'll check the flights when I get back to the office.'

Daisy hugged him one last time. The cradle started to descend again, but she gesticulated it away. Three steps up the ladder, she took a moment to wave to her good friend. *'Be safe and well, Anton. We'll talk in a few days.'*

He watched as she made the open door, dropped inside, turned and waved again, her legs still dangling over the side until the far more sensible Aidan dragged her into a seat. Someone pulled the ladder up, and the chopper rose into the air, and then turned in the direction of the Kenyan shore, and was gone.

He let out a deep sigh, stood and watched until the helicopter was out of sight. Then he turned and sighed again, as his eyes took in the devastation that was once his weekend home. Daisy was right, it was all her doing.

But it was far from her fault. He couldn't see anything wrong in fighting for family, and fighting for justice for two total strangers who deserved it. Everyone he liked and respected had come out if it in one piece, and that was what mattered.

Property could be rebuilt, and live again. People couldn't.

Chapter 42

Love is a Many Splendored Thing

The British army cargo aircraft wasn't as comfortable as the Emirates flight that had flown them to Uganda just over a week previously. But the crew had been briefed about their secret return cargo, and had rigged up some makeshift seats in the empty hold.

The vast space which held nothing more than a few boxes of bits that were being returned to the UK, and four humans who were hitching a lift, felt cavernous. But it didn't matter. They were going home with one extra passenger, and that meant everything.

Celia was asleep. As soon as the rescue helicopter had reached Laikipia air base, two female Kenyan nurses had whipped her away, given her several doses of benzodiazepines, together with something to help her sleep, which had worked better than anyone expected. As the morning light came, and still three parts asleep, she'd been helped onto the British transport aircraft, and then, assisted by the comforting drone of the engines, had fallen fast asleep even before they'd reached the North Africa coastline.

Daisy, sitting next to her, gazed at her with eyes full of a mother's love. 'Look at her, dear. She looks so thin.'

'She was always thin,' smiled Aidan, sitting on the other side of Celia. 'But yes, she needs a little of my gourmet cooking therapy.'

'You might have to cook rather a lot, Dip.'

'Whatever it takes, Flower. I know there's a long road ahead of us, but there's a light at the end of our tunnel now. With a lot of love and TLC, we'll all get there.'

Sarah nodded her head. 'You two are up to it. Awesome respect to you both. You never gave up… and we might have left our mark on Uganda, but it was worth every minute.'

Daisy narrowed her eyes. 'I wonder what happened to the general.'

'He's most likely in Rwanda or somewhere now, living in a mud hut, unable to sleep for fear someone's going to kill him,' said Aidan.

'I hope someone does,' Sarah growled.

Daisy found a cheeky grin. 'So what do you think of Uganda, Sarah dear?'

She shook her head, but smiled at the same time. 'Well, I could say it was so exciting, but maybe it was the kind of excitement I could do without.'

- - -

One week later, Anton Kowalski watched as the heavy door swung open, and a small, white-haired man appeared, shielding his eyes from the late-morning Ugandan sun. He looked back momentarily as the door thudded shut behind him, and then cast his eyes to the Volkswagen sitting fifty yards away.

Anton climbed out, waved to him. *'Joseph!'*

The elderly man walked slowly over. 'Mr. Kowalski? They said you would be here to pick me up. But why?'

He grinned. 'It's Anton, please. Let's just say I wanted to put the lid of closure on things, in the best possible way.'

216

'They tell me you had much to do with my release. I wish to thank you. But I had thought Florence would want to be here to collect me.'

'That's my fault. I persuaded her to let me do it. She's waiting for you, so get your butt in the passenger seat, and let's not keep her waiting any longer.'

Anton pulled into the brick-weave driveway of Michael's home in Ntinda. Florence's Toyota was parked up against the garage door. Joseph let out a deep, emotional sigh.

'My son had a nice house. I feel so unhappy he is not here to enjoy what he created, all because of me.'

'I can't disagree, it is indeed tragic. But what you have to remember Joseph, is that you fell foul of an evil man, and you knew if you didn't keep your mouth shut, both you and that little lady waiting for you wouldn't be here now.'

'I know, Anton. But it is still not easy to live with.'

'But you are living, Joseph. And you owe it to your son's memory that you enjoy the rest of your time to the full. That's what he wanted, after all.'

Joseph nodded. 'I cannot argue with that.'

'You ready for this?'

He sucked in a deep breath. 'Yes, I think so.'

They walked to the front door, and Anton knocked loudly. No one answered, so he knocked again. There was still no answer, but then someone appeared around the side of the house. Florence walked slowly up the steps to the porch, never taking her eyes off Joseph. Her face showed no emotion, masking the hundred emotions trying to burst out of her.

She came to a stop, four feet from her husband.

'Joseph.'

'Florence.'

'You silly, stubborn man.'

'I had to protec...'

He didn't get any further. As the tears rolled down her cheeks she fell into him, and he wrapped shaking arms around her, held her in a tight embrace they'd not been able to enjoy for fifty-six years.

Anton stepped back a little, feeling like his job was done, and not willing to intrude on their private reunion he had no further part in. Lost in their embrace, neither said a word. 'Be happy, you two,' he said quietly, and turned to leave.

Florence finally broke away from her husband, called out to him. 'Please, Mr. Kowalski, don't go. I have prepared a little food, on the terrace. A celebration. Please join us.'

'It is kind of you, Florence, but I will say no. Today is for you two, not for someone who is a total stranger.'

Florence shook her head, smiled to him. 'I think you are not a total stranger. At least take tea, and do not insult my hospitality.'

It was said with no malice, but Anton knew he actually would insult them if he did not stay a little longer. He nodded, followed them as they walked hand in hand to the terrace, where what looked like a feast had been laid out on a table under a big green parasol.

Florence disappeared into the house, and reappeared three minutes later with a tray of milky teas. She handed one to Anton. He sipped it thoughtfully, and then spoke to his hostess.

'I gotta say, Florence, General Oyite met his end in a very ironic way... some would say a fitting one.'

She wouldn't look at him. 'I would include myself in those people, Anton.'

He chuckled. 'Guess we'll never know who threw that grenade into the command hut at Entebbe barracks, hey?'

218

'I suppose we never will.'

'Yeah, and whoever it was kinda knew the authorities wouldn't spend too much time trying to discover who it was.'

'As you say, it was indeed an ironic way for him to lose his life.'

Anton bid them farewell, and told them he would do all he could to make sure Joseph received compensation for the extra years he'd spent incarcerated for the crime that never really was.

Joseph shook his hand, Florence gave him a hug, and he left them to their private and heartwarming celebration.

As he drove away, a smile broke across his bushy face. It had been a good day, and a fitting lid had been welded forever onto a pot that stank worse than a soldier's boots.

Daisy and her crew had inadvertently shaken a few leaves off branches, and exposed the bare wood of a very old tree. The authorities were no doubt relieved they were safely back in England, and unlikely to visit Uganda again.

But he couldn't help a wave of sadness wafting through him. Doing his thing with an old friend had brought a strange kind of forgotten excitement, one he never thought he would experience again. He would miss the thrill, and miss every one of them, even though their visit had left him without a weekend home!

But none of that could dampen the smile on his face. Despite it all, he couldn't stop one thought running riot through his head.

In so many different ways, love was indeed a many splendored thing.

———

We hope you enjoyed Daisy's third adventure. We will be eternally grateful if you can spare two minutes to leave a review on your preferred site. It really is very easy, and makes a huge difference; both as feedback to us, and to help potential readers know what others thought.

Thank you so much!

Follow Daisy's adventures in the Fourth One, 'Pirates of Great Yarmouth'

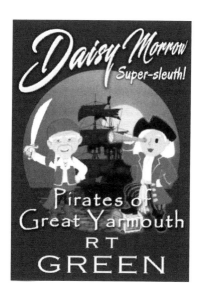

An old business associate of Aidan's invites him, Daisy and Celia on the inaugural two day cruise of a replica of the 'Black Pearl' he's built, Captain Jack Sparrow's ship from the

Pirates of the Caribbean movies. Daisy, of course, is a little curious (or suspicious) of the Russian billionaire's motives

for inviting them, and it's only a few hours after they've set off from Great Yarmouth when they discover she's all too right to be suspicious. Of course.
'Pirates of Great Yarmouth' is a modern-day swashbuckling adventure, where the seemingly-innocent turns out to be anything but. Of course!

A sneaky preview of the Fourth One –

Pirates of Great Yarmouth

Chapter 1

'Is that me?'

'It was taken when you were sixteen. I had it framed after you were… gone.'

'I do remember it, kind of. Looking at it now, it feels like I was someone else, watching myself being photographed.'

Daisy smiled, put a loving arm around Celia's shoulder. 'It will come back to you. Give it a little time, and then you'll know for sure you're you.'

She was sitting on the bed in the room Daisy had made for her, the small framed photo of the three of them in her hands, her slightly-misty eyes transfixed onto it. It had only been half an hour since they'd arrived back at the cottage, waved goodbye to Sarah and the taxi which was continuing on to take her home, and wandered wearily into the house.

Celia was still more asleep than the others, but within fifteen minutes of arriving at her new home, she was asking where she would sleep. Daisy had taken her upstairs to the room they'd furnished for their daughter, even though they hadn't known if she was still alive, or if she would ever use it.

She reached out a hand and wrapped it around her mothers'. 'I can't believe you moved here and made a room for me... just in case.'

'It's called faith, dear. Although I will admit there were times it was hard to keep it.'

'I'm sorry, mum.'

Daisy pulled her into a hug. 'No need for that. None of it was your fault.'

'I'm getting vague flashes of things though... like before I was taken... when was it?'

'Just over three years ago.'

'Before I was taken... I feel memories that weren't so nice. But I can't actually see them, like they're in a fog.'

Daisy kissed her on her head. 'Now isn't the time to dwell on what happened back then. In a day or so, when you get used to your new surroundings, and if you want to, we'll jog your memory together. Right now, I want to enjoy just having you home safe.'

'Me too. It's a nice house; cosy somehow. I just wish I didn't feel like I could sleep forever.'

'Would you like to sleep now?'

Celia nodded. Daisy walked to the wardrobe, pulled open one of the doors. 'You may not want to wear any of this stuff anymore, but we kept all of it. For when you came home. Right now it's all you've got, but when you feel up to it we'll hit the shops in Kings Lynn.'

'Thanks, mum. This is all a bit… overwhelming.'

Daisy hugged her again. 'Take your time. There really is no rush. Snuggle up, and your father and me are only in the next room if you need anything.'

'Thank you. For everything. I'm still not sure what you did apart from kidnap me, but something tells me it'll be jaw-dropping news when it comes.'

Daisy headed downstairs, her heart singing, but aware one string was slightly out of tune. Before she'd left Celia she'd noticed her body was starting to shake again, part of the withdrawal symptoms from whatever it was Emmanuel Oyite was pumping into her for three years, to make sure she stayed a willing submissive.

The Kenyan medics had given them a supply of stuff to help combat the effects, but that was way short of enough fire-power in the long term. Much bigger guns were needed to fight the battle, and they were needed quickly.

'She's happy for now, dear,' Daisy said as she flopped wearily onto her stool at the peninsular unit in the kitchen area. 'But we can't fight that particular war alone.'

He handed her a large brandy. 'No, I realise that. It's early evening now, but tomorrow we'll get on the PC, find a good clinic to get her detoxed.'

Daisy lowered her head. 'We've only just got her back, and I'm going to have to wave goodbye again?'

'Only for a couple of weeks. We can't do this without an expert helping hand, Flower.'

She let out a faltering sigh. 'I know. I wish I'd accepted that before Celia was taken. Now there's an even longer road ahead of us to defeat this particular villain.'

224

He took her hand, tried to smile some encouragement. 'Yes, but look on the bright side... everything we took to Uganda might have ended up exploding into a billion fragments, but the most precious thing of all didn't, and came back with us in one piece.'

'Just about, Dip.'

'So now it's down to us to make sure those pieces stay together.'

'You always were too sensible, dear.'

'Enough for both of us. But now it's seven in the evening, and we've just flown back from Africa in a less-than-comfortable transport aircraft. That bed of ours is screaming at me to fall into it. You mind if I do?'

'I'm right behind you.'

Still trying to force herself awake, Daisy wandered into the kitchen to find Aidan making coffee. Just about to wish him good morning, the patter of tiny feet on the gravel outside the kitchen door stopped the words forming.

It wasn't hard to work out there were four tiny feet, accompanied by two slightly bigger patters. A key was slipped into the lock, and the door opened to reveal the vision in polyester that was Maisie, with Brutus on the leash by her side.

She looked a little surprised she wasn't alone, to say the least. *'Daisy? Aidan?'* she stuttered.

'Coffee, Maisie?' Aidan grinned.

'What are you doing here?'

'Well we do live here,' said Daisy.

'But you're not due back for another four days... I think...' The short, slightly-portly woman counted on her fingers. 'Yes, four days it is. I was coming to water the plants, like you asked.'

225

'Let's just say we got done what we had to a little sooner than we expected,' said Aidan as he handed her a mug.

'But you said it was a holiday.' She took the mug, thanked him. 'Brutus is thirsty, can he have a saucer of milk? Semi-skimmed, mind you.'

Aidan shook his head, put the saucer of milk on the floor as Maisie unclipped the lead. The hairy furball looked grateful, even though once again he was the cat that didn't get the cream.

Daisy tried to offer an explanation for why they were back early, but was reluctant to go into too much detail. It *was* Maisie after all, who tended to need a little more careful explanation than most. 'It was a holiday, but there was another reason we went to Uganda as well.'

'Really? I don't suppose you're going to tell me tho...' The words trailed away as the reason they went to Africa wandered in, rubbing her eyes.

'Morning guys... oh, hello, whoever you are.'

Daisy grinned, even though she wasn't looking forward to the somewhat complicated introductions. 'Celia, this is Maisie. She's a bit nuts, but a really good friend.'

'*Daisy...*'

'Maisie, this is Celia, my daughter.'

'Huh?'

'My daughter, Maisie... you know, fruit of my loins and all that?'

'I know what a daughter is, Daisy. I just didn't know you had one. Where have you been keeping her all this time?'

'We keep her locked away in the cellar. Looks like she just escaped.'

'Mum...'

'Daisy, I might be dozy but I'm not stupid. You don't have a cellar.'

226

Daisy, unable to resist winding up Maisie, said something she likely shouldn't. 'Ah... it's a secret cellar. No one knows it's there except us.'

'Mum...'

'Oh I say... but isn't it illegal to keep someone locked away like that?'

Aidan was still shaking his head. 'Maisie, Daisy is just winding you up... again. We didn't lock our daughter away, but we did go to Africa to bring her back.'

'Oh I say. That takes a bit of believing, Aidan.'

Daisy put a hand on Maisie's arm. 'Actually dear, the truth is Celia was kidnapped three years ago, then trafficked to a Ugandan general who drugged her to keep her a submissive, then we got a clue about where she was from a Nigerian thug who subsequently died, so we went to Africa to rescue her and almost caused an international incident, but we escaped to an island where we got shelled by Howitzers which destroyed the home of an American hillbilly, then we were rescued by the Kenyan air force and flew back home in a British military transport aircraft.'

Maisie narrowed her eyes, and then grinned and batted her hand in front of her face. 'Daisy dear, if you're going to pull my chain, at least come up with something vaguely believable!'

'But it's the truth.'

Maisie shook her head and turned away. 'Perhaps you'll tell me what really happened one day. But I still can't see where the secret cellar fits in...'

She grabbed Brutus, ready to take her leave. Celia's sleep-filled eyes saw the furball for the first time. 'Aw... you've got a cat... *on a lead?*'

'Oh yes, dear,' said Maisie as she clipped the lead back onto his collar. 'He loves it when we go for a walk around the village. He's so good on the leash, and it stops him chasing the dogs.'

Celia glanced to her father. 'This village seems like a very *interesting* place to live, dad.'

Maisie, much more switched-on than it first appeared, picked that up straightaway. *'Dad?* Now I'm really confused. Aren't you two just good friends?'

Daisy groaned. 'Maybe we'll just say we're friends with benefits... like a daughter.'

'Oh I say!' Maisie trotted through the kitchen door, the obedient Brutus by her side. 'I have to go now, before I get even more befuddled.' She disappeared, shaking her head. They still heard her parting words though, just before she went out of hearing range.

'Daisy Morrow and Aidan Henderson... well I never...'

Celia narrowed her eyes at her mother. 'Morrow... isn't that your maiden name, mum?'

Daisy groaned silently again. 'Dear, it's a long story. Shall we have breakfast first?'

Aidan picked up a small stack of post from the entrance hall just inside the front door, as Daisy tried to explain to Celia the reasons why she'd reverted to her maiden name when they moved to the village.

He came back into the kitchen, sorting the six letters in his hands. One of them was an A4 envelope, and as he looked at it curiously, he let out a chuckle.

'Dear?' said Daisy.

He showed her the envelope. She read the words printed right across the front. *'Open this if ye dare?'*

Aidan decided he was brave enough, and slid out a rectangle of stiff card with three pieces of paper attached to it, printed to look like old parchment.

'We've been invited to an all-expenses-paid two-day cruise on a pirate ship, dear,' he said quietly.

Daisy read through one of the invites. 'It's from Ilya Komanichov. Wasn't he the Russian tycoon you fell out with... what, twenty years ago?'

Aidan nodded. 'Yes, Just before I retired from the accountancy firm sixteen years ago, I voiced my suspicions to them that he was expecting us to... shall we say, be too creative with our accounting. They subsequently expelled him as a client.'

'And now he's inviting you on some kind of jolly?'

'Perhaps he wants to show me there were no hard feelings. It didn't exactly affect him... he's an oil billionaire now.'

'I know. He bought the rights to explore an oil field off the Norfolk coast, which came good. Made him a fortune once they started pumping the oil out.'

Aidan was reading the smaller print on the invite. 'It says he's built a full-size, fully-functioning replica of Jack Sparrow's ship, the *Black Pearl*, from the Pirates of the Caribbean movies. It's got twenty guest cabins, and he plans to operate it as a cruising hotel, recapturing the spirit of the pirate life.'

'For a small fortune in pieces of eight, no doubt. A bit like the one at Disneyworld, but this version actually sails.'

Celia was reading through her invite. 'It says the inaugural cruise departs from Great Yarmouth, and ends at its permanent home in London Docklands. And everyone on board has to wear pirate dress.'

Aidan smiled. 'It's four weeks from now. Maybe we should go, see it as a bit of therapy for Celia? Well, for us all perhaps.'

Daisy narrowed her eyes. 'Must confess I quite fancy waving a cutlass around for a couple of days.'

'Oh dear, dear. I forgot about the cutlass part.'

'Tell him we'll be delighted. But I'm a little curious as to why we're invited, after all this time.'

'Let's just try and have an adventure without mortal danger involved for once, dear?

———

COME AND JOIN US!

We'd love you to become a VIP Reader.

Our intro library is the most generous in publishing!
Join our mail list and grab it all for free.
We really do appreciate every single one of you,
so there's always a freebie or two coming along,
news and updates, advance reads of new releases...

Head here to get started...
rtgreen.net

Printed in Great Britain
by Amazon